A Natural Born Witch

By Megan Blacke

Published in United States by

Megan Blacke
Advisor Garage LLC

© Copyright 2015 – Advisor Garage LLC

Table of Contents

Contents

Chapter 1

The Bookshop of Horror's door rattled but refused to give. The person outside challenged it with panicked hands, pounding then shaking the door knob, like it would make a difference to the locked and bolted door.

They were wrong.

The door was silent. Different sounds replaced the shaking from behind it.

I strode through the closed shop, grabbing my bathrobe tight, stumbling as I jammed my feet into the fluffy slippers my father had given me last birthday. The idiot still thought I was ten years old but thankfully he'd dropped the Princess phase only three years after I had.

I stared at the now silent bookshop door.

It stared back, with no apology for waking me up at this ungodly hour.

Cursing under my breath, I stumbled towards it.

"I'm coming. I'm coming." I shouted at whoever was on the other side of the still door, dragging the bolts across.

With a strength I didn't know I had I wrenched the door open, "Do you have any idea what time it is? You had better be dead or dying to wake me up at this time of night..."

I readied some choice swear words. They died on my lips as my senses screamed; assaulted by the tangy smell and what seemed like buckets of blood emptied on my doorstep.

Fighting down a dry-heave, I started forward, this wasn't some sick prank, a woman was slouched amongst the gore. Wide eyed I looked at her petite hand still holding onto the door handle, dangling and disconnected. It fell on my slippers with a red bounce, leaving a mark, like a child's potato print.

Kneeling, ignoring my knee threatening to slip in the pool of congealing blood, I frantically tried for a pulse amongst the torn up rags and torn up women, my fingertips probing and panicked.

Shivering, feeling like it was taking hours, I found her cooling neck. Pressing down on the artery like I'd been taught, I felt a brief flutter answer my touch.

Then it, and she, were gone.

Chapter 2

"Hells teeth" I mumbled under my breath, passing a bloody hand through my short black hair and letting myself fall back to sit against the door frame.

I took the deepest breath I could, really pulling it in like it would clear my nose of the smell of death.

Looking over the red bundle, I examined the day with tired eyes, just daring it to be nice. Still dark outside but only just, the night was seeped away like it was ashamed, wanting to avoid me, the crimson edges of daylight fragmenting like the pool of blood at my feet. The poor girl's time of death - 3am.

My feet squelched, eyes were pulled to the floor, the sheer volume of blood amazed me. A gunshot wound? A mugging?

Then my fried brain remembered the dismembered hand, the artery must have emptied out all eight pints. Noticing the girl's neck where my fingers had checked for a pulse. It was gapping open, a thin edge gash smiled obscenely up at me.

My hands were bright red and bloody. Crap, I was covered - my robe, slippers, even my pajamas were a mess but it only half mattered - I was alive.

Turning I noticed my front door, deep slashes ran top to bottom, a forearm's length at least. Coming from the side more slashes crisscrossed the first set like a crazed game of tic-tac-toe, the boxes filled with a girl's blood splatters instead of zeros.

Sucking in a breath I tried to steady myself, my eyes gyrating rapidly from side to side of their own accord. I took hold of the doorframe, needing the support.

What was I dealing with here? The hand, the sheer quantity of blood, the deep groves sliced into my door. Wide eyed I realized this wasn't a mugging gone bad, this was something else entirely and was on a whole different scale.

This was screwed up sick psycho murder. I'm sure the cops would have a better way of putting it then me but I didn't – some sick bastard had carved this girl up like a pig at a Sunday roast. And it had happened on my doorstep.

Chapter 3

This is probably where I point out that I had a cursed or was perhaps blessed, depending on your point of view. I have a smattering of what some would call 'Power'.

Now that's not to say I can make a light bulb glow just by holding it, I'm not a person sized Duracell battery but I am, what some might call, a witch.

Yes a witch - but don't say it to my face if you want to remain boil free and don't fancy the idea of owning a tongue that can catch flies twelve inches away and your vocabulary being limited to the word 'ribbbbbit'.

I went down the few steps to the street below and started to caste out, search with my second senses, the thought, the gesture and the word.

My energy fizzled like lightening being grounded during a storm. Kicking the sidewalk and stamping my foot in frustration, there was too much fresh blood and violence for my power to be effective.

My chances of discovering anything using the power that my regular senses couldn't were smaller than a flea's reproductive organs.

As I started to walk back up to the shop, a rhythmic clacking echoed out from the damp streets, the waning moon reflected off stray puddles. Looking around I tried to see what was making the noise, it stopped just as quickly and as elusively as it had materialized.

Making sure I didn't move her I went back inside, a heat burning between my shoulders blades as I turned my back on the street. Flicking a look over my shoulder the street was still empty, even though I knew without any doubt, it wasn't.

My first call was to my Father, my second the police. Having dealt with the important stuff, I took a nonchalant walk into the bathroom, strolled across the small tiled room, ran a hand through my short black hair,

took a nice leisurely breath and puked up my guts.
　　 I just loved Mondays.

Chapter 4

My Father sat at the kitchen table, a steaming cup of dark tea held between his hands, watching as the cop on the wrong side of heavy chewed the end of a pencil before flipping back one more time through his note pad, sheets flying.

"So let me make sure I'm getting this straight." He paused, a brief smile struggling to lift his jowls. "You heard knocking at around 3am. So about three hours ago?"

I nodded.

"You answered the door and there was a dead person on your doorstep. Is that pretty much it Ma'am?"

My Father caught my eye before I answered, a question in his face, wondering if he should jump in and be my big Daddy protector or if I would resent his interference.

Poor guy – it must be tough being the single parent of a seventeen year old girl. He never quite knew what's was the right thing to do or say. No wonder he didn't say much. Probably safer that way. I love the clumsy oaf, I wish I could explain it to him but most of the time I didn't know myself until after I'd already reacted or probably more accurately, over-reacted.

With a side to side jerk of my head he went back to staring into his hot beverage concentrating on the curls of steam.

I turned back to the cop.

"No need to call me Ma'am Officer. My name's Sam. Sam Ray. But yes, that's exactly how it happened. They wouldn't quit knocking, I dragged myself out of bed, put on a robe and by the time I got to the door everything was quiet. When I opened it, they were already dead or as good as..."

He looked me up and down, taking in the black

ensemble, the short black hair, dark red lipstick like the queen from Snow White, and my crimson bodice with hooks from top to bottom, black velvet skirt and leather boots. I considered apologizing for not looking normal but screw it, I'd taken too much crap growing up to be apologetic now. What can I say – I'm a Goth without the grunge. Call me crazy and don't bother inviting me around for tea and cookies if you give a crap but it's who I am. Don't like it, tough.

Using the pen he scratched his head, then went back to sucking on it. I truly wished he would just get to the point.

"Officer Trublood?" I said with my sweetest voice. Out of the corner of my eye my Father flinch making me smile, he knew.

Trublood didn't, he smiled like a friendly puppy responding to a pet name. "Yes Ma'am?"

"I have spent most of my life being dragged around one naval base or another. Me and my Father are it Officer Trublood, the total family unit, I've dealt with more than my fair share of bureaucrats and bureaucracy. If there's one thing I can spot faster than a Navy nurse can spot pubic lice it's when I'm being jerked around by one of those shit kicking bureaucrats. Now I'd appreciate it if you'd get to the point so I can get on with my day..."

By the way his eyes locked on mine I could tell I'd just lost any chance of getting my friendship Brownie Badge from Officer Trublood. Oh well, I'd survive.

"Sorry Ma'am. Wouldn't want you to be inconvenienced or have you go out of your way to help the police solve a murder investigation would we?"

I guess he did have a point but that didn't mean he could waste time with me when he could be looking for the slime that created sushi from the girl whose blood I still needed to wash off my doorstep.

"So how can I help?" with a smile that almost needed to be nailed to my face. "I've told you everything just as it happened." I said trying not to sigh.

"Tell me again why you were sleeping at the bookshop and not at home?"

"We..." I started to say but Officer Trublood interrupted, raising his pen in a silent question. Rolling my eyes I revised my statement. "We, my father and I, arrived in Salem and took over the Bookshop less than a week ago. We're due to open in a few days and I've been working to get the place ready. It was way late; I couldn't keep my eyes open any longer, so...crashed here."

"Any friends come by after you finished up?" He said glancing from me to my Father and back. "Maybe a sneaky beer or two? A little puff perhaps? Maybe a small party? Things got a little out of hand?"

I bit back a smart assed remark. A cop sees a kid dressed different, black dyed hair, black fingernails, maybe a little makeup and assumes there's some weirdness of one kind or another going on. Guilty until proven innocent.

"What? ...and after the party we filleted a door to door salesperson that called at the wrong time, like 3am then we called the police just to make life really interesting?" I said sarcasm dripping off each word "If that's really your going in premise to this crime then..."

"So no party then?" a tinge of disappointment in his voice.

"A party? Chance would be a fine thing. Like I said just a minute ago, we've been here less than a week. I haven't had an opportunity to get plugged into the local Salem Trench coat Mafia yet?"

"Trench coat Mafia?" He asked, leaning forward like he was finally hearing something interesting.

"Forget it. Just a bad joke" I said, trying to keep the disdain under control and failing miserably. Me and my big mouth, my Father was right, I needed to learn when to keep mine shut. I snapped my lips together and resolved to keep them closed until my twenty first birthday.

Trublood must have sensed my new Monday morning resolution as he prodded his pen behind his ear, flipped his pad shut with a snap and disappeared it inside his jacket as he strolled from the kitchen and began to walk towards the door. He stopped.

Like a well-rehearsed kids party magician his card was between pink sausage fingers in front of my face.

"Call me if you remember something new. I'll be in touch again soon." With a nod he pulled open the door, charms hanging from the ceiling either side dancing and ringing, "Oh and Ma'am......" a slight sheen of sweat on his face from the effort.

"Not Ma'am. Sam. Sam Ray." I automatically corrected then grinned. "Let me guess...don't go taking any out of state trips anytime soon?"

My smile dropped onto the floor as he nodded.

"Glad we see it the same way" Trublood said shrugging apologetically like it wasn't anything to do with him.

"Great. Welcome to Salem. America's Bewitching Seaport" I said to his creased back as it disappeared out of the shop.

Chapter 5

My father was still captivated by his tea as I entered the kitchen and began tidying. Picking up and throwing a dishtowel in the general direction of the towel rack before I knocked the tea spoons into the sink and Trublood's cup was pitched in with a smash.

"Doesn't seem a good cop that one...but..." My father spoke before taking a quick sip choosing to ignore the ceramic chips passing in front of his face.

"You're telling me" I said, ratcheting up in volume as I made more motions of tidying without actually doing it.

"So this...this weirdness. Anything to do with you then Sam?"

My mouth must have just fallen all the way open because the back of my throat felt the draft.

"Are you mad? How can you even ask me that?" I shouted, throwing breakfast plates into the bottom of the sink and following them with my Father's half full teacup.

He sulkily watched his hot tea swirling down the plughole.

"I blame myself" he said shrugging.

"For what?"

"Well, if I'd been around more. You know. Been a better Dad. @Not been so focused on the Navy. Spent more time home then maybe..." He said, his voice trailing off.

Hearing his self-reproach took the boil off my anger. I said sitting down next to him, my arms around his waist. "Maybe what?"

"Then...well, maybe..."

"What? Come on...Spit it out..."

"Well then you wouldn't be...

"What? You can't even say it can you?"

He hung his head, his chin on his chest, silent. I couldn't help myself, I jumped in with both size nines stomping.

"Then I wouldn't be a...a...witch? Is that what you can't bring yourself to say?" I demanded standing up fast, my chair falling back and clattering against the kitchen floor.

We'd had this discussion before. Too many times. Being a witch wasn't his fault, it was no one's fault and it wasn't such a bad thing anyway. It was just who I was that's all. But that didn't stop me from being pissed that he didn't get it.

Blowing my fringe I reached out to him, my hand touching his shoulder. I knew who he really blamed and it wasn't himself or the Navy.

"Nana Tottot was as close to a mother as I've ever had. She was a kind, special old lady who helped me see who I was that's all."

He leant his head against mine. "But you're never going to be just like everyone else. Average."

I pushed him away a little so he could look into my eyes.

"Who wants to be average Dad? Do you? Is that what you want for me? Average."

He seemed to consider it but only for a moment, shaking his head from side to side, his hands wide as he tried to explain, eyes pleading.

"No...I never wanted you to be average but I also didn't want you to be..." he swallowed. "...to be completely abnormal either. I mean...a Goddamned witch Sam..."

I filled my cheeks with air and counted to ten before blowing out my captured breath, doing my best to ignore the 'abnormal' word that I accused myself of being when the bedside light was switched off.

I tried again even though I knew it was hopeless.

"Nana Tottot was a Suruhana, a healer. On the Islands everyone knew she did good works not bad...she looked after me when you were away. She taught me how to use what I am, what I have. If I'd been average then nothing would have happened, she would have just been my baby sitter, nothing more - it wasn't her fault any more than it's yours that I'm not average."

His head kicked up as that evil little thought wormed its way in.

"My fault?"

I shrugged, honestly not knowing if it were true.

"Well I get it from somewhere. You, or Mom, somewhere. It sure as hell wasn't from living under an electrical Navy pylon since birth. Don't suppose you took part in any Navy experimental drug programs you haven't told me about have you?"

He laughed but the fact that my powers may originate from him made him noticeably paler.

"My fault?" He said raking his fingers through his hair. "But your powers Sam..."

"Are just that Dad. They're mine. And I can use them, they're mine and I'm in control. You know me, you know what I'm capable of and what I'm not. You helped make me so trust me okay?"

He gave me a small grin, a look so typically Dad that all I could do was hug him. Then I took a breath and faced the real question.

"Dad? That person on our doorstep..."

"Yes?" He said, moving me at arm's length to get a good look at me as I spoke.

"...the doorstep girl, she had nothing to do with me. I need you to know that. Nothing at all."

"You're sure? Trublood doesn't see it that way."

"Well Trublood can kiss my..." I interrupted before Dad interrupted me back. He went on regardless.

"...He knew...he sensed there was something you hadn't told him, some piece missing from your story."

"And is that you sensing Dad? Now you have powers?" I said grinning, the potential hurricane blowing out of both of us, catastrophe averted this time.

He smiled back. "Well like you said, you got them from somewhere".

"Yeah. But it sure as hell wasn't from you Commander." I punched his shoulder. "I blame Mother."

He stopped smiling. Shit, now where did that come from?

That was a subject guaranteed to stop the

conversation. Standing he crossed to the sink turning on the faucet to wash the remnants of his tea away.

"Maybe it was", he said sulkily.

Now why did I have to say that? Did I think he would act differently this time? Wouldn't clam up or avoid the subject? That he would do a hundred and eighty degree turn and tell me why she left, why she hadn't been back since I was a little kid too young to remember more than just a fuzzy outline.

I looked at his thin lips squeezed tight. Nope. Not this time either.

Leaving the kitchen and I heard him open the door from the apartment and enter the Bookshop shop floor the sound of opening boxes and stacking books hard onto their shelves started a moment later.

Walking into the shop I watched him overly concentrating, the conversation over.

Had it been my idea or my Father's to buy this bookshop with his early retirement money? My father, the owner of the Bookshop of Horror in Salem MA? Boy would his Navy buddies piss themselves if they knew that.

That image of my Father didn't fit even to me but I'd spent seventeen years following him around, it was about time he did something for me. He knew it so here we were in Salem Mass.

He was happy because he got to live close to the sea and I was happy because I got to run the Bookshop of Horror and finally grow some roots. A big chunk of my life had been spent outside of the US in Puerto Rico and Guam. So where else would a returning witch want to live but in Salem?

With a frown I turned to take a look at the Bookshop door. I felt its accusation reminding me of last night and the unsolved murder. Questions formed unbidden - Who the hell had gutted sliced and diced her? Did it have anything to do with me and Dad? Why had I kept the clacking noise I'd heard from Trublood or made sure he took a real good look at the scratches on our door?

Maybe because I hadn't figured out what the noise was and telling him would have been as helpful as a Barbie band aid to the girl.

I also didn't fancy telling Trublood or my Father I'd seen scratches just like that before. Information like that without some rational explanation would have marked me out for a padded room with no ocean view and sleeves that did up at the back.

Did the murder and those cuts have anything to do with me, Nana Tottot and Guam? Were my old mistakes catching up with me?

I needed to get some answers and didn't have the first idea where to start.

Damn! I really hated Mondays!

Chapter 6

Before we go any further I'd like to clear up any false impressions you might already have after listening to my Father. My Father is Navy through and through, cut him and he'll bleed salt water instead of blood. We've lived outside of the United States for a hell of a long time and most of my life was spent on Guam, one of the most beautiful Islands in the middle of the Pacific Ocean perched between the Philippines, Japan, and the United States.

My Mother left us when I was still in diapers and my Father has always been too busy to explain his side of the story. In my head I've made up a thousands of my own to explain why she left. I stopped believing the one about Princesses, Trolls and Unicorns when I was eight, the other nine hundred and ninety eight I discarded a few years after that. The one that stuck, she left because she didn't love us anymore. Yeah, that one worked.

Perhaps my earliest memory is of Nana Tottot feeding me juice dripping Papaya. She was my Nana and we spent hours together. Even as a young kid I knew she was special, I'd trail along behind her, holding onto her skirts and giggle at the people bowing, tipped hats and other signs of respect she and indirectly I, received. She expected this respect and was never disappointed as we walked through the villages on the Island. I swear I must have walked across the Island a hundred times before I was ten years old.

And why did we spend so much time walking through the villages?

As well as being my Nana (her most important job) she was also a Suruhana or healer. She was a descendent of the ancient people of Guahan and was north of seventy herself. As I'd drop off to sleep she'd tell me stories about the Island and its people. As I grew I pestered her about being a healer. Nana told me about the power we have within ourselves given to us by nature – we are all special you just have to let it get free.

My Father has never really understood. It's not that he's wrong exactly...it's just that he's got a more, shall we say, modern view of these things than me. The Chamorro people have lived on Guam for over six thousand years. The Chamori had healers and Magi, drawing their power from nature and watched over by their ancestors. These ghosts watching over them were of an ancient people who arrived before time, taking the name of Taotaomo'nas, ancestors of the Land. When the land was still a garden.

So even though my Father's views are pretty antique and less enlightened than I'd like, his views are still modern compared to what Nana Tottot and in turn, I believe. By just being close to nana I learnt and begun using the power and my second senses.

One of the first lessons Nana Tottot taught was every living being emanates a force field and leaves behind traces of itself as it moves through the world. There was still a chance that whatever had been outside the Bookshop had left some kind of impression I could sense if I opened myself to it.

The thought of lowering my defenses anywhere close to where that women had been cut apart again was not appealing. I mentally slapped my own face. Tough luck Sam, you needed some answers.

I'd promised my Father that the murdered girl had nothing to do with me, witchcraft or my powers – truth be told, I wasn't one hundred percent sure I hadn't just unknowingly lied my cute ass off. One way or another I needed to start understanding what the hell was going on. So here I was, my leather boots planted firmly in the nearly dried pool of blood I'd refused to wash down. The patch looked black but where the blood had pooled it was still wet and sticky looking. Without thinking I crouched down, my fingers gently touching a tiny wet section in the middle.

A physical force like a slap across my face hit me as my fingertips brushed a line through the murdered person's lifeblood. My cheeks smarting, involuntarily sucking in a breath, shivering to the soles of my boots.

The temperature all around me dropped to past freezing, breath clouding out, hitting the smooth surface of the wooden door, a hidden imprint of fingers spread and sliding now visible from the condensation. The murdered girl had been knocking, thumping, demanding I open the door, her heart complaining in fear and then something cut her up. My breath showed her last act, her hand reaching out one last time before she finally gave up, her fingers sliding down the door as she raised a hand to protect herself.

Opening up my mind, I sensed her pain, the cuts that burnt, her icy fear and then disgust at the evil force that had stood here. My nostrils flared as the memory of the beast returned, tickling the hairs of my nose and making me want to sneeze out the smell of the creature that had stood right here as the girl breathed her last.

My shivering turned into mini-spasms as I tried to resist, forcing my teeth together so they wouldn't chatter as I trembled from my very center. I couldn't resist it, I was in the dark, pushing hard against the door, I'd been running, my heart, pulse and breath so loud in my ears. Open, open, open. I smashed at the door with the side of my hand it shook but stayed closed, resolute. The entity stood over me, blocking out the light from the street lamps, a dark space in my vision, a hand or maybe a claw held high, the moonlight glinting. A slow slash became more, faster, faster, life force draining.

Falling back my eyes snapped open, severing the link. Heart pounding, my breath blowing in and out I felt like I'd been hit on the base of my skull with a hammer, a sharp pain shooting through the back of my head. Sparkles and white dancing lights of a mega headache appeared shortening my already limited breath.

God. This wasn't just some street thug robbery gone bad, this was an attack of pure evil, a hunger to kill and tear. Calming down my breath I sat for a few seconds, wanting nothing more than to feel the breeze, untangling the memory traces from my own. I tried to filter through everything seen, felt and smelt. It was all jumbled and didn't make too much sense but one thing I did know for a fact, I'd unknowingly lied to my Father.

This attack had been about good and evil, about death and darkness. It may not have been directly related to me but it was linked to magic. That was just a stomach sickening, head aching fact. I couldn't ignore it had happened and go on with my life, it's not who I am. Not how Nana taught me to be. She would never back down from fighting the darkness and neither will I.

Whoever had used Dark Magic on my doorstep had just screwed up. Big time. I was going to make them regret it. Nana Tottot wouldn't have accepted anything less of me...

Chapter 7

The sign for Griffin's Bookstore swung gently from the two small hooks. Unlike my Bookshop of Horror, this was a serious bookshop, exuding dust and tradition.

Maybe it was the gold lettering, perhaps it was the floor to ceiling bookshelves visible through the grimy windows, the lack of razzmatazz or street marketing. Come in if you want or go somewhere else, either is just fine with us.

No plastic tarantulas, fake cobwebs and tombstones here but if I wanted real answers I doubted I'd find it nestled between Lovecraft and Lumley. I needed to get serious. Serious research meant a library or a really good bookshop – Griffin's Bookshop.

Pushing my way in a small brass bell tinkled and interrupted a conversation between two old folk that stood by the money till.

A fifty something red grey flecked haired man with a goatee looking like some English country professor with the required bow tie and tweed jacket pushed half-moon glasses up his nose to get a better look at his visitor.

I tried to think non-intimidating nice girl thoughts as he considered how I was dressed and what I might want and failed miserably. It still blows my mind that a seventeen year old with a bit of eye makeup and black nail enamel can look 'scary' to anyone over fifty, people that have lived through wars and more but there it is – we do.

Surprisingly his expression didn't revert to a frown or nervousness but settled into interest and warmth. Well hell, maybe Salem wasn't so backwards after all.

"Yes Miss, can I help you?" He said, coming out from behind his desk walking around the white haired lady that he'd been talking with.

"Um yes – I'd like to look at any books you may have on local folklore and superstitions please."

His face lit up, a nice big smile as he put a finger to his lip considering the best place to start out our search.

"As you can imagine we stock quite a few books that cover the different facets of that subject – we have a number other tourists have found particularly informative..."

"Ah well erm, I'm not looking for general background on Salem and the witch trials – this is more for...research".

He raised his eyebrows, looking surprised but I could tell he was starting to get interested and so was the lady he'd been speaking with. She turned and for the first time I locked eyes with someone who could have passed for Nana Tottot's sister or cousin. She didn't look like Nana. She was as white American as they come and Nana was a native of Guam. Physically they were complete opposites, but there was the same strength of character and an indefinable power running through them like they were made from human titanium. I could see and feel the strength of her even from the other side of the store.

Her eyes twinkled at me as I stood speechless, then gently nodded like she knew me and was welcoming me to the neighborhood. Icy blue eyes shone out of a wise face not because she was old but because she was a lady who knew more than she was telling.

Walking across the shop, she held her hand out. I took her small dry hand, it felt like I was coming home, a warmth traveling up my arm making me feel like I was standing in a beam of sunshine coming through Griffin's bookshop window.

"You're the new lady with the Bookshop of Horror. Welcome to Salem."

It was a statement not a question. She knew exactly who I was even though I hadn't had a chance to introduce myself to anyone since we'd arrived in Salem.

It wasn't that I was being antisocial or anything but we were on a deadline to get the bookshop ready in the next couple of days. Since arriving in Salem each of my days had been exactly the same - wake up, throw on whatever was close and not too smelly, stock shelves with the books we'd bought at auction until we couldn't lift books anymore then sleep and start over.

"Yes, that would be me. Sam. Sam Ray. I'm afraid I don't know who...?"

"I can't imagine that you're afraid often dear" She smiled at our first private joke and gave my hand a squeeze. "I'm Louise Conrad. But you can call me either Louise or Grandma Conrad. They work just as well."

"And you can call me Sam." I said, feeling a little discomfort at being called 'Dear'.

"Of course Dear." She said turning to Mr. Griffin, his shaggy moustache centering a pink roundish face. "And this is Mr. Griffin. So you're interested in local folklore." She said, an eagerness in her voice.

I looked from Mr. Griffin to Louise Conrad and made up my mind about them. Walking over to the counter, I took up a pen, a brown paper bag and sketched.

"This mark was left on my door early this morning."

I held the sketch out to them. Louise was the first to move, taking the brown bag and bringing it up to her face. She hummed before passing it to Mr. Griffin.

Lowering his eye glasses I watched his expression as he examined my multifaceted tic-tac-toe.

"Someone left this scratched on your door you say?" Mr. Griffin said as he gave it back to Louise.

"I didn't say that it had been scratched but yes...it was gouged into my door and looked very much like someone had used a hunting knife. It was deep and ragged."

He nodded, chewing on one arm of his eye glasses as he gave his head a scratch then Louise, their eyes connecting, gave him a brief nod.

"You both know about this don't you?" I said.

Mr. Griffin cleared his throat as he walked to a bookshelf, his fingers running gently over the spines of various books. Finding the book he'd been looking for his index finger pulled it forward.

"This is a good place to start." He said "Here".

I jumped as he tossed it to me, my eyes wide as I scrabbled to catch the book and not let it fall.

Turning it over a picture of a wolf grinned at me like it found the whole subject highly amusing.

I looked up at both of them to see if they'd started laughing yet. I read the title.

"Werewolves, Witches and Wraiths? You've got to be kidding me?"

Louise reached out and took the book from my fingers.

"Why would we be kidding Child? You can't honestly stand there being what you are and tell us you don't believe in werewolves and wraiths? Why would there be one and not the others?"

My heart skipped a beat. She knew. The old baggage knew that I was a witch but how the hell...

'Yes, I know exactly what and who you are young lady...' a calm and pleasant voice said in my mind as Louise offered the book out to me.

'Now that's just...freaky. You're in my head...' I thought back to her, taking a few steps back, my back pressed against the glass door out.

Looking over my shoulder it was still broad daylight and people were walking past the bookshop, the world seemed to be going on just as it was supposed to. I shook my head.

Louise unbuttoned her cardigan rolling up her sleeves.

"I'm sorry. I didn't mean to surprise you but if you didn't have the power then you wouldn't have heard me – to be honest I didn't really expect you to either hear or answer. And I thought a little louder than usual because it isn't every day I'm referred to as a 'baggage'. We have a lot of catching up to do. I recommend you take that book home, read it and come for tea tomorrow afternoon. Shall we say 3pm?"

I didn't know what to say. The baggage...I mean...Louise, er, Louise was another women of power and she's trying to tell me my home has been marked by a wraith or a werewolf. What the hell had I got myself into, coming to Salem?

Mr. Griffin glanced between the two of us still chewing on the arm of his glasses.

"Can I?" I waved the book at him.

"Of course" he said without hesitation.

"There's something else you both should know..." I said.

Louise raised her hand, her mouth downturned, her sadness obvious.

"We already know child. A poor wretch was left for dead on your doorstep. Not a good omen for your new beginning in Salem. Perhaps before coming to tea tomorrow you can have a chat with the authorities?"

"The authorities?" I said.

"Yes – given the location they may be inclined to share facets of the case with you that they wouldn't share with other members of the public. A call to Trublood perhaps?"

They knew Trublood was the cop on the case and it had only happened early this morning.

"Is there anything you don't know?"

"Yes dear. I can assure you the list of what I don't know is many times greater than the list of what I do. So, can we expect you for tea", a warm smile flitting across her lips as her sleeves were rolled back to her wrists.

"3pm. I'll be there."

"Good. Until 3pm then De.." Louise said.

"Please don't call me Dear..." I said heading her off.

"No Dear."

A moment later I was standing outside, Louise and Griffin invisible through the window. Now that lady was a feisty one. I could tell this was going to be interesting.

I re-read the title of the book grasped in my hand - 'Werewolves, Witches and Wraiths'.

I turned over what Louise was hinting at, werewolves or wraiths running around killing people during the darkest hour of the night. A large cloud slid across the sky and passed in front of the sun, a cold breeze tickling the hair at the back of my neck.

Shuddering I pulled my own cardigan across my bodice and watched the tips of my leather boots appearing and disappearing beneath my black velvet skirt as I walked towards the town center cursing the fact that I had books sitting in boxes that were not getting put on their bookshelves.

Chapter 8

Having been in town less days than fingers on my two hands I hadn't yet had time to explore Salem. Father and I had made the decision to move to Salem almost sight unseen. The Bookshop of Horror had become available, we'd bought it and here I was, outside of the Salem Police Station, nervous as all hell.

Most self-respecting teenagers have a healthy respect and nervousness for the police...it's not so much that we have guilty consciences but if parents represent authority, then the Police are parents on steroids, authority to the max...any surprise they make us a little nervous? Saintly kids, good kids, bad kids, any of them would be standing here with big jar worth of butterflies zipping around inside their stomachs.

So I did what most kids do when feeling this way. I pulled up my metaphorical trousers, got some attitude and before I knew where I was at, the sarcasm fairy has come to town to wave its wand across my tongue. See ya Sam Ray nice girl, welcome Sam Ray Bitch on wheels!

Pulling open the glass door I led with my chin and strolled through like I owned the place. A cop close to my Father's age sat at a desk raised to eye level.

Engrossed in his paperwork he had failed to notice my entrance or my Sam Bitch stance, leather boots shoulder width apart, my hands on hips head thrown back.

What a waste of a great entrance. Deflating like a field full of hot air balloons at the end of a long day, I waited a few moments, back to normal size and shrinking fast. I coughed, hoping to get his attention before I ceased to exist in any form greater than a puddle of embarrassed slime on the linoleum floor.

I was invisible to him, this guy knew how to turn the thumb screws or had teenagers of his own, he knew exactly how to burst our attitude bubbles, he had it down to an art.

Without looking up he finally deigned to speak, a strong Boston Irish accent which made him sound a little sarcastic to my ears. Damn him.

"Yes Ma'am. How can I help you on this bright and beautiful day?"

"I'd like to speak to Officer Trublood if he's available."

"Humm and who might you be missy?"

"Missy?" I said, my voice going half an octave deeper. He was getting dangerously close to resurrecting Sam the Bitch if he wasn't careful.

Now he looked up, a smile sparkled across his bright blue eyes, knowing he was pushing all the right buttons but strangely he looked at me not my hair, the makeup or the clothes. Yeah, this guy definitely had been through the teenage boot camp, no question. I needed to resist the desire to scratch his eyes out otherwise he'd have won this round.

I put on my nicest smile in answer to his.

"I would appreciate it Sir..." I paused to let that sink in, licking my dry lips briefly. "...if you could let Officer Trublood know Sam Ray is here to see him. I believe he's in the Criminal Investigations Unit."

"That he is Ma'am. If you'd like to wait on that bench over there" pointing at the seat bolted into the gray painted cinder blocked wall, "...I'll see if he can be disturbed. Now this is important business you'd be bothering our man with no?"

Giving him my most somber nod I spoke as gravely as I could while keeping my face straight,

"Yes Sir...very important business. None more important I can assure you".

"Well alright then. I'll be right back". He said, getting down from his chair.

"And I'll be right over there" I said, pointing at the bench.

"Yes you will" He said with a leprechauns' grin.

Licking my index finger I marked an imaginary 'One' in the air as he walked towards the door leading back into Police station.

His face cracked with a big smile and a nod in recognition of the end of the battle but not the war.

Round one to Sam Ray. We both knew it. One for the girls.

Chapter 9

"Miss Ray. What can I do for you?" Officer Trublood was speaking before he got all the way into the waiting room, jacket off, tie loose and pulled to the side, hair ruffled. Walking head down he was in a tired hurry wearing the same clothes he'd worn creased at out last meeting at 3am. I was probably just who he wanted to see.

"Sorry for bothering you. I hoped you might have five minutes."

"No bother" he lied badly, "Have you remembered anything ...new...since we spoke this morning?"

"Can we go somewhere to talk? Just for a few minutes?"

He seemed to think about it, then straightening out his tie, ushered me towards the blue door that lead inside the station.

A few half asleep street people staring into the distance while a cop ignored them behind a large blue and gray counter.

Trublood made conversation as we walked through. "This is the booking room. If you're spending time in here then you're probably in deep sh..trouble".

We arrived at a wall of cinder block with a row of evenly spaced doors all colored with the Salem Police station blue. There must have been a sale on at the closest Paint store.

He ushered me in, I peeked my head around giving the room a good side to side, it was a scarily plain room except for three chairs, a table and a nice big microphone perched right in its center. None of the walls had their structure compromised by any such frivolities as windows and we were so deep inside the station, windows would have looked out onto more cinder block. The interview rooms was illuminated by a solitary florescent tube light enclosed within its own metal cage. Lovely.

This was a really bad idea.

Swallowing I tried to hide my nervousness with a flick of my head, strolled in like I already knew my way around, hopefully looking a hundred times more confident than I felt. Trublood tried to keep his face straight, who was I trying to kid? Him or me?

I mentally took back the 'one' I had marked up back in the waiting room. I had just lost my single point to home turf advantage and we hadn't even started a real conversation yet. Whatever I had thought I'd be getting out of this conversation was going to be a real challenge. If I managed to leave this room without confessing to every crime that had happened in Salem even before I'd been born, would be a good result.

Alright Sam, that's enough of that I could hear Nana Tottot laughing at me for getting myself into this mess but she'd be expecting me to stand up straight, make the best of it and face my nerves with courage. With a long breath I turned to Trublood who was closing up the door behind him. It was then I saw the door didn't have the same handle as on the other side. The door would only be opening if Officer Trublood unlocked it or someone on the other side felt like letting in some air.

"Is it necessary to lock me in here Officer Trublood?" I said trying to keep my voice calm.

He raised his hands, "Sorry, that's just the way the doors work. Don't worry, unless I die of a heart attack, I can let you out any time you want."

"So now if I want?"

His face colored a little, a little purple passing across it, his jawbone twitched just before he shrugged.

"Sure. If you want".

I shook my head. "I'm used to being outside a lot. This place is a little..."

"Claustrophobic right? Yeah well it's designed to be functional while being a little intimidating. It helps us get the job done..."

I pulled the plastic seat out from the table with a groaning scrape. "I can understand that".

"So why are you here Miss Sam? Have you

remembered something new?" He said, pulling out his own seat, dropping himself and letting the chair catch his exhausted body.

"I've remembered a few things now that I've had a little time to calm down."

He leant forward, "Go on..."

"I heard a noise, it was close, just after the girl stopped knocking. I heard it as I was opening the door."

Officer Trublood gestured with his hand urging me on.

"Sort of a clacking sound. Rhythmic."

He leant back in the chair and pulled his tie back to the side. "Rhythmic like how? Music? Can you be..." he stuck his little finger in his ear giving it a twist "...more specific?"

I swallowed, not wanting to go out on a limb but I was half committed so I may as well go all the way.

"Not like music. I didn't immediately pick up on it, but when I did it sounded like a person dragging a metal object along a wall or floor, like it was clacking against the cracks in the sidewalk."

Trublood stood, scratching his head before he took the back of his chair in both hands, leaning on it silent as he thought through what I'd told him.

"Who was she?" I asked hoping Trublood would feel accommodating enough to share.

"She was just an ordinary girl."

"Was she robbed? Raped? Sorry to ask but I'd like to understand what happened this close to home. You can understand right?" I said, hoping my question would seem natural.

He blew out a breath pushing himself away from the chair, I could see the cogs working as he consider how far he should go.

"Robbed? No. Raped? No thank the Lord. But...and this is to stay in this room if you know what's good for you Ms. Sam." He locked his eyes on mine until I showed some sign I understood. With a nod, he continued. "She was cut up badly and it wasn't a regular knife attack, there was a lot of anger and fury in it. And it they didn't use just a knife...we believe they used multiple knives. The wounds suggest they were strung together, evenly spaced...like fingers."

The butterflies that had been happily flitting around inside my stomach turned into acidic worms of vomit threatening to make a dash for the freedom of the interview room floor.

"And her hand?"

"Its early days but we believed she was trying to protect herself. Just brought her hand up and the knife or knives passed through and followed onto the jugular. She stopped knocking for two reasons. Her hand was gone and her life-blood had sprayed out. She was either dead or close to it before you even opened the door. There was nothing you could have done Ms. Ray."

Holding my hand across my mouth I focused on my breathing, taking in deep breaths as my mind's eye went back to those moments. The bundle of bleeding rags, the coppery smell, the faint pulse as I reached in.

Without realizing, Officer Trublood had moved beside me, his hand gently on my shoulder. I just as gently shook it off.

"I'll be okay. You said she was just an ordinary girl. Who was she?" I said.

Trublood walked over to the door. Interview over. He held up a key ready to open the door.

"We don't know who she is Miss Ray. She had no identification. Do you mind me asking if that's your natural hair color Miss Ray?"

Wow where did that come from? What the hell did that have to do with anything?

"I don't see what that has to..."

Trublood raised his hand, the sentence dying in my throat.

"This is probably nothing and it only occurs to me now after seeing you in daylight. In fact it's nothing. Forget I even mentioned it. I'm just tired, I should have known better."

Now it was my turn, a second later I was standing with my hand resting on his arm, silently urging and needing him to tell me whatever he was trying to avoid saying.

I answered his question. "I have red hair."

He nodded. "I thought so. The girl..." he swallowed, something stuck or not sitting right, "...she was about your age, your build, with black hair and red roots. Now I've seen you in the daylight, you could pass at a stretch for Sisters or easily Cousins. You don't have any family in Salem?"

My hand fell to my side as it sunk in. Shaking my head I managed to mumble, "No. No family at all." I looked up at him, "should I be worried?"

With a bad reassuring smile he unlocked the door turned and offered me his card for the second time in one day from the pocket of his sweat stained shirt.

"It's probably nothing Miss Ray. We don't get these sorts of happenings in Salem. The last time we had something unpleasant like this in Salem it involved burning people at stakes." He smiled, "Seriously there hasn't been one murder in Salem in the last ten years or more. It's something of a record in Massachusetts."

He opened the door and I walked past him, I could smell sweat and nervousness. Biting my lip and tried to push down the thought jumping up and down demanding attention inside my head.

"That Massachusetts record you're so proud of was broken this morning Officer Trublood" I paused standing on tip toes so I could look at him as close to level as I could "...when a women who looked a lot like me was cut into big pieces".

Trublood pulled the door closed keeping his eyes on the floor but I could see his lips thin and straight.

God, he was doing a lousy job of reassuring me, he really didn't have much practice at this...

Putting the card in the folds of my skirt, I let him lead me through the different corridors of the police station. The lack of air pushed in on me, it was all I could do not to turn my quick walk into a run. A sweat brook out across my forehead I concentrated on my breathing and walking. In out, in out, left right, left right.

On the sidewalk I kept on walking, not stopping even to recognize the time officer Trublood had given me or the concerned look from the desk sergeant. Their eyes drilling into my back from the doorway of the police station as I crossed the street and started the walk back to the bookshop.

Officer Trublood had been worried.

I was just plain scared. Worried would be a blessing.

There was just one thing that made me feel better when something spooked me...

Chapter 10

I had managed to get home without being mauled, killed, sliced or diced, so it was a good day. Perhaps I was worrying for nothing. Then I remembered the feeling I'd had when I had opened my senses to the last moments of the young girl's life. The anger and fury of that person slashing down at me, at her, made me glance repeatedly over my shoulder, my skin literally crawled as my mind's eye pictured the slashing.

The tool glinting as it was raised high. I wanted nothing more than to rush home, throw my keys across the kitchen, run to my room, pull the curtains tight down and hide under my bedcovers until whatever hurt her was locked away, dead or just plain wandered off.

So much of me wanted to be normal, to let someone else deal with it. Dad maybe or Nana, anyone but me. But no, hiding wasn't me. I wouldn't let it be. But God it would be so easy, if only I didn't have to give up part of myself to be that other person.

Not changing the subject but if you ever flick through one of those tourists books about Guam you'll see bright color photos of a truly beautiful Island, all the bikini and buff holidaymakers with perfect white smiles. Like a Disney commercial without the big black mouse ears.

What the books and postcards don't tell you is, you have to be tough to live and survive in Guam. It's an Island thirty miles long by eight miles wide smack dab in the middle of the Pacific Ocean with nowhere in particular to the North, South, East or West.

Over generations the Islanders have got used to the fact that their survival is on nobody's shoulders but their own.

When a challenge comes, you deal with it yourself and ideally keep it in the family without bothering outsiders. So when the Typhoons of life hit, the people of Guam have no one to turn to but themselves and maybe their own neighbors. That might be why there's a problem with bullying in schools, blind eyes are turned by teachers and parents, it's seen as a necessary evil to toughened up the weaker kids and make them self-reliant. In my experience, the only time a teacher will get involved is when a kid ends up in the emergency room. Even then it was a 'maybe'.

I hadn't been a weaker kid, I made the other mistake, I was different. Being brought up by Nana Tottot, trying to hide the developing power made that an absolute clear cut certainty. There's no point crying over spilt blood, all I can say is Nana Tottot and eventually my Father came to the conclusion that learning a martial art would come in useful. After a few good poundings from too many kids at once in the school bathrooms I readily agreed with them.

That had been eight years ago. Since then I made sure I spent three hours each week training and practicing, minimum. I'd even grown to love the time spent away from everything – school, my power and even my Father. When you were in the zone your mind couldn't be anywhere else. If you were lucky, it all just fell away.

I'd skipped my usual training since arriving in Salem but if Officer Trublood's unspoken but sledgehammer clear suspicions had any reality in the real world, then I'd not be ready.

I'd use my fear as a motivator, to get up and get on with fixing the problem, fear would be a positive, not a paralyzing negative.

If someone tried to sushi my butt then they'd find their teeth travelling at speed down their throat to meet their testicles travelling forcefully from the opposite direction.

I may be cute but that didn't mean I was going to be anyone's victim.

Chapter 11

Flicking on the light switch, my stomach jumped into my throat as the bulb in our back room apartment blinked then popped leaving me in darkness. Swearing under my breath I felt my way through into the kitchen, wondering where the hell the spare bulbs were. Dammit.

Tripping over something my brain unfroze reminding me the bulb in the hallway was just one bulb. What an idiot I am.

Shaking my head I felt along the wall and found the kitchen switch. The light in the center of the room glared making me blink and scrunch up my eyes.

You see. That's what fear does to you. Stops you from thinking, makes you panic. I pulled open the kitchen cabinet a solitary cardboard rectangle from the previous owner sat dusty in an otherwise empty cabinet. Maybe there was someone looking out for me after all. Wiping it off I held it up to the light, the filament intact. Yes, there is a god, maybe even two.

I had to face it, part of me was afraid. Hell, all of me and my imaginary friends were afraid.

The conversation with Trublood had hit me more than I realized. And I still hadn't told him about the scratches on the door. Sure I'd told him about the noise and maybe he'd noticed the scratches himself.

But maybe he hadn't.

He looked it over at what? 8am in the morning.

He'd focused on the body, the puddle of blood, the hand. For all he knew the scratches had been there before. I knew better. He didn't.

Damn, I should have said something but the conversation with Mr. Griffin and Louise had made me keep my mouth shut. Until I'd had a longer conversation with them and got my head straight, I was going to keep quiet. Sure. That's what I do. It was a plan.

He was a policeman, he was trying to help.

But having made up my mind, I felt better.

Looking around the kitchen I made up my mind about something else. I needed to blow off some steam and be back before it got dark.

Maybe I should also call Dad and see if he wanted to come over and keep me company tonight. I'd call him later, but first training...

Leaving the kitchen I walked through to the room masquerading as my bedroom.

A black futon which had belonged to my father in his early navy days and now had the good fortune of being mine. Caught midway between being a sofa and a bed, and made a valiant run at being both, a split personality piece of teenage furniture that seemed perfect for me. It was the only clue this was a bedroom and not a storage room - Bags, boxes and cases piled high against one wall, my private space even more of a disorganized shambles than the shop.

Poking out from beneath the futon was my workout bag bulging with focus mitts, shin guards and bamboo kali sticks. Now maybe this is where you and I part company...a girl punching bags, kicking pads, sparring, getting covered in sweat. Well if that's the case so be it. It really would be nice to think I'd always be able to call on someone big and strong to protect frail little old me. Hey maybe Daddy would always be there to come pull my covers to my shaking chin, smooth my hair and chase away the nightmares. Yeah, exactly.

Those days passed us by like coke in glass bottles, Stepford Mothers with cotton pinnies and teenagers who still thought 'E' was a letter between D and F.

So yeah, at a time of crisis I could yell loud with all my fingers crossed or I could learn to look after myself, and know, deep down, that I'm as ready as I can be if it ever does...just in case. Sure I'm a witch, always have been, always would be, but hexing people with a bad rash was not going to help during that spur of the moment, instant reaction crisis. But hopefully my fists and legs would.

Besides which I enjoy the punching, kicking and

sweating - so there. Dragging my bag out I hung it over my shoulder and like Elvis, left the building.

Chapter 12

Every training facility is different. There's no cookie cutter design, they all have nuances that reflect the master who started them. Despite similarities to my own school, walking into this one reminded me I was a long way from the Island.

Sure it had the usual posters of past masters, weapons like ornaments, the kick bags and mats which, even now were being used by sweaty enthusiasts. But it still wasn't my school and the faces turned in my direction with a shared recognition I was a stranger drove it home. Inclining my head forward, a slight bow to all, recognition I was entering new territory and although we had a common interest, I still needed to be invited.

Letting my bag drop to the floor I stood, feet apart waiting for the welcome wagon.

Faces went back to what they were doing,

And, as I watched, a person nodded to his partner and broke away, walking towards me in bare feet across the shiny blue mats. He was close to twenty, Hispanic and maybe about one hundred and eighty pounds coming to just above my shoulder. Was this his place? He didn't look old enough.

Never letting my eyes leave his, I nodded. He returned it.

"Good evening, Miss?" He said, a slight Latin accent coming through even in those few words.

Maybe it was the black hair, the skirts and bodice but I got the feeling he wasn't taking me seriously. Why don't people get beyond what's on the outside? Putting my head on an angle I looked him over, resisting the urge to turn my butt around and walk out.

"I'm new to Salem. I'm looking for a school to train at."

He smiled, tried not to chuckle as he looked me up and down making no effort to hide that he found me amusing. Call me short tempered but stepping forward on the matt I placed a foot to the side of his own, grabbed, turned and pivoted.

A second later Mr. Macho was on his back looking up at me, a shocked expression on his round face as he gave his head a scratch where it had hit the matt, as I gently rested my foot on his chest. I was trying hard to keep a smile off of my own face, hell, why bother. I gave him my biggest grin.

Perhaps smiling too soon, he took a hold of my toe and heel and twisted my foot fast. But I was ready. Forced to twist, my other foot came around aiming for the side of his head. Seeing it coming he rolled onto his side releasing my foot and sprung up. Damn this kid was fast. Faster than I'd seen before.

I sent a punch straight at his chin. Expecting him to slap parry it away or at least move his head out of the line of fire but he didn't bother. My fist slapped solidly into his palm and lost all energy as he held it firmly in place. He raised his other hand in mock surrender.

"Hold it Miss. Okay, so I'm sorry okay. You just didn't look like you knew your way around a fighting mat. Thought maybe this was some kind of school prank."

Blowing my fringe off my head I rolled my sleeves up my arms and stood back, keeping my fists tight and raised.

"What is it? The clothes? Hair? Makeup? What?" I said.

He shrugged, "Yeah sure, all of the above. What do you want me to say? So I'm a guy that judges a book by its cover. You'd think I'd know better right?" He grinned, but this time it was the friendly grin, I could tell he'd put the sarcastic 'what the hell am I looking at' grin firmly back in its box.

Sometimes it helps to kick butt.

What can I say, I'm just cool.

I lowered my guard but stayed on the balls of my feet in case he finished the joke off with a nice throw to the matt.

"So is this a good place to train or not?" I asked.

He puffed his chest out a little, "None better. This

is the place to come if you're serious. If not, I'm sure you'll find a school that will take you."

I raised my hands into a fighting stance. "Do we have to start over short stuff?"

"Damn you're feisty Lady" he said, getting a laugh out of him. With that he went from pain in the ass to friend, he offered his hand as a sign of welcome and peace.

"Sorry. Sometimes my mouth gets me into trouble. The names Raul, my friends call me Benito. "

I took his hand, his grip forceful without being painful. He wasn't proving a point, he just a naturally strong guy.

"Sam. Sam Ray. So you want to spar?"

He grinned scratching his head where it had hit the matt. "Thought we already had".

I blushed a little, embarrassed, "Yeah, but this time you can have padding so I won't hurt you too bad".

Laughing he took my bag and placed it beside his, "Whatever you say Sam. Let's go."

Ninety minutes later, battered, bruised and happy, we had finished putting each others' fighting styles through their paces. Raul was good and hadn't been joking about taking his training seriously. When he was off the mat he was all jokes and mouth but as soon as he stepped onto that mat, the joker was gone and he treated his training like his life depended on it. He was focused, serious and his reactions were incredibly fast.

Grabbing my pads and gloves Raul walked over, he'd thrown on a hoodie, a woolen beanie and a pair of boots at least two sizes too big for his feet, laces flapping.

I tried not to stare as he slipped a backpack over his shoulders finishing off the urban skateboarder look. Hey, if I wanted people to look below the surface of my Goth stuff - the bodice, velvet skirt, leather boots and jewelry then I needed to do the same.

"Need a walk home Sam? It's getting dark outside..."

I looked out of the window surprised that he was right, the sun disappearing below the horizon the day over, early evening already. Dammit, I'd been longer than I'd planned and I'd forgotten to call my Father. But I wasn't going to tell Raul I was nervous, not after spending the past hour earning his respect.

I put on a positive face and shook my head.

"You're offering to protect me? Didn't I just kick your ass around the mat or do you have a smaller brain and shorter memory than I thought? Maybe I cracked your head harder than I thought?"

"Hey Miss Defensive. Why don't we just say that this is my neighborhood and I just want to make sure someone as pretty as you gets home without mishaps. Not everyone's like me you know. There are some real jerks out there." His grin broad as, without waiting for an answer, he picked up my gym bag.

This is usually the point where I tell the pushy guys to go to hell, take my bag back and sashay out of the room with my nose up in the air. I even considered it, but as I stood there my mind pulled open my front door, smelt the tangy blood, saw the gapping flesh, heard the clacking. Two was better than one, biting my bottom lip I let him keep my bag.

Now don't get me wrong, I really had been kicking Raul's rear end around the training mat, or even if I'm a little more honest, I'd at least given as good as I'd got but there's some reassurance in numbers. Even if that number is two and I barely knew him. Maybe this was a bad idea on top of a big pile of bad ideas in my life but at least he was a known quantity...

"Sure, you can walk me home but no funny ideas. This isn't a date or anything. Just friends taking a stroll is all..."

Raul sniggered, hanging my gym bag across his shoulders. "Don't worry. I don't date Goths. Even tall cute ones. But it's good you're already thinking of me as a friend. I'm making progress. Sure and steady progress..."

"That's not progress Raul, its sympathy". He

sniggered as he pulled my bag tighter over his shoulder and set off out of the gym.

A few strides later and I'd caught up with him, if he thought I'd trail along behind him he had another think coming...

Chapter 13

"So how come I haven't seen you around before?" Raul asked as we walked down Washington Square West, looking out over Salem Common, people wandering through on their way home.

A trolley clattered along in the street, reminding me of the sound I'd heard just after the girl had died, making my flesh creep.

Trying to cover up my lapse I ran my hand through my hair blowing my fringe, "Sorry Raul, I have a headache. What's the question again?"

He glanced my way, his step faltering before picking up its natural bounce again.

"Salem. When did you get here?" He said trying again.

"Just a week ago. My Father and I took over the bookshop."

This time it wasn't my imagination, his rhythm changed as he walked beside me, keeping his head down as he spoke under his breath.

"Which bookshop?"

I could hear the tension in his voice, like marbles grinding between his teeth.

Turning to look at him he kept his eyes locked on his feet and the floor as we walked.

"Why Raul? This is getting a little weird you know? What difference does it make...?"

His shoulders hunched as walked beside me hands pushing deep into his front pockets, the bounce gone from his stride, other things on his mind.

"It makes a difference Sam. Which bookshop?"

Raul turned, giving me a glance so fast I almost missed it, I got a really strong feeling he was afraid I'd see something in him he didn't want to show. The way he was acting was really starting to freak me out, imaginary fingers tip-toed up my spine and gently brushed against the hairs on my neck, the night suddenly much darker than five minutes ago.

I stopped and realizing he had little option, Raul stopped too, hesitant to look up at me, rearranging the beanie on his head moving from foot to foot.

"What the hell Raul. This isn't funny, we barely know each other and you're freaking me out...that's just shitty."

I'd had enough, I was out of here.

Turning I stamped my way down the street, focused on the red orange pathway thankful cars were driving past keeping me company.

A hand reached out grabbing my elbow.

Half expecting it I whirled grabbing Raul by his hoodie and ramming him against the wall. In spite of himself he grinned, raising both of his hands up in surrender. "Peace Okay. Jeez, is this how you treat all your boyfriends?"

"Only the ones who play stupid games trying to scare me as we're walking home. I've had twenty four hours of hell and the last thing I need is more crap. You have something to say, say it."

His hands dropped to his side as he nodded,

"Sorry Sam. It's been a pretty lousy day or so for me too. I wish I could tell you about it but..."

"Yeah, sure, whatever..." I said trying to keep the disgust out of my voice as I turned away.

"Wait. Look just wait okay?"

I turned back. "What for? So you can jerk me around some more?"

Moving back against the wall he smoothed out his shirt, checking himself over, giving himself some time. I watched him clenching his jaw, realizing he had made up his mind. No matter where it led.

Chapter 14

Trying not to tap my foot like a petulant kid I gave him some room.

"Well?"

"You just took over the Bookshop of Horror right?" he said watching me.

Biting my lip I nodded, not trusting myself to speak.

"Shit. I thought it was you." Raul said.

"What the...what do you mean 'you thought it was me'? We haven't even opened yet."

He hesitated way too long. "Well how many girls look like you? All I'm saying is I've seen you a few times that's all."

"Look Raul. I've know you less than a day and even I can tell you're lying your ass off. Either you're a really lousy liar or you want to tell me what's on your mind so...what the hell is going on? Is this about the girl?"

His head snapped up from staring at the floor.

"What girl?" his voice low.

"You don't know?"

He kept his mouth shut so I filled the silence.

"A girl was murdered outside the Bookshop early this morning. She was..."

"...cut up, torn apart..." Raul said finishing my sentence, his glazed eyes looking nowhere as his legs seemed to give out, he slid down the wall. I crouched, shaking his shoulder to snap him out of it.

"Raul, for Christ sake. Raul..."

Jumping up he shoved my hand aside his hand going behind his head.

A moment later he whipped out a skateboard and dropped it with a clatter to the orange tiled floor.

"I'm sorry Sam. I have to go."

"But..."

"Sorry. I'm really, really sorry..."

"But..."

He skated away, board knocking against the edges of the evenly spaced tiles until he turn a corner onto Essex street.

I crumpled against the wall until I was cross legged on the sidewalk.

Feeling like I'd been punched in the gut I sat there with my arms around my stomach. Shaking my head I tried to tell myself it was all in my imagination, but I couldn't fool myself.

Sucking in a breath I force myself to stand, the sound of his skateboard fading, punching over and over into my psyche.

There was no other sound quite like it. A skateboard travelling across a sidewalk. Jumping down a curb. It was totally unique.

The last time I had heard it a girl lay dead at my feet, her throat torn out, her hand cut from her body.

Realizing how close I had been to the same fate I swallowed down a throat of bile.

I needed to be strong. There was no way I was going to get through this if I wasn't...and smart. And fast too.

Chapter 15

What next?

My Father?

Officer Trublood?

Louise Conrad?

Telling any of them I'd heard a skateboard after the girl was murdered would generate a raised eyebrow or a slightly interested 'really?' I mean come on, how many axe murdering psycho serial killers have you ever heard skateboarded from a slashing blood bath?

Yeah, just as many as I had...a big round zero right?

So it was ridiculous right?

Raul had cut the girl into cubes then jump on his trusty skateboard, switch on his MP3 player and slid off into the early morning sunrise listening to some tunes?

Kind of unbelievable right? Right?

But what now?

Was Raul involved? There must be thousands of skateboards in Salem. The chances it's Raul are just...madness. It's madness.

But he acted so weird when he found out I lived at the bookshop, he flipped out.

I started to walk. Breathing deeply, despite the time of night feeling a little reassured as plenty of cars passed by and up ahead the Hawthorne Hotel with people popping in and out all the time. I'd be fine.

Arriving where Hawthorne Boulevard splits, I took the left fork knowing it intersected with Derby Street and would take me to the bookshop.

I was nearly home.

My neck itched.

I gave it a scratch, feeling a slight prickle.

For the first time in my life, my second sense opened of its own accord, reaching out around me, looking for danger without an order from my conscious brain.

A threat was close.

Casting out a net of awareness I touched it, the darkness, the hate, the animal fury and it hit me like a knife shoving deep and hot into my forehead. It was intense, bloody and dark. It smashed against my consciousness like a wave crashing through tissue paper, unable to resist I crumpled, my mind going blank before my body hit the ground.

I leant on my elbow, willing myself, forcing myself, up. Then I saw the shadow, the glint.

Feet scuffling.

I tried to look around.

More exhausted than I've felt in a long time I lay my head against the floor, not caring about the grit on my cheek, unable to move.

Eventually a pair of boots walked closer, just inches from my nose, they stopped.

A hand reached out and with my last ounce of strength dragged my nails deeply across the back of the hand.

With some degree of satisfaction I saw the hand pulling back sharply, briefly seeing small bleeding tracks from the scores of my nails as I heard a deep growl.

With my last conscious breath I allowed myself a small smile I was no Bruce Lee but I'd still drawn first blood.

Take that you...

Sam signing off.

I was pitched in blackness.

Chapter 16

It hurt.

They hit me.

My face stung.

Snapping my eyes open I pulled back the impenetrable curtain on my mind, my Father's face came into focus, his palm pulled back. So that was it.

"Alright pop enough of the 'wake the broad up with a good slap' Okay? It only works in the movies. Do it again and I'll call social services" I smiled, more tired than I've felt in a long.

His concerned face relaxed a little but his hand stayed floating by my face unsure what to do with itself.

"Er Dad. Hello. Hand? Child beating is still against the law in Massachusetts so why don't we just sheath that Puppy okay?" looking at it out of the corner of my eye ready to block in case he was still running on concerned Daddy autopilot and went for strike three.

He lowered the lethal weapon, slowly but surely. I was out of the danger zone.

Running the back of his knuckles gently across my cheek he looked at me with his big concerned eyes.

"Fancy telling me what happened?"

As my last memory was lying unconscious and completely unable to defend myself I wasn't sure myself. How the hell had I got here? And where was here?

I looked down, I was still in my gym clothes and smelt a little from the workout, a forest of stacked books in every corner. I was home.

Running my hand through my hair I bit my lip chewing it a little. The last thing I needed was an over protective Father locking me inside the Bookshop and throwing away the key until my hair grows long enough for some wayward prince to use as climbing equipment.

But I didn't have a clue how I got from Hawthorne Boulevard to horizontal in the Bookshop. Where to start?

Watching my face he was almost reading my

thoughts. Sometimes it sucks to have a parent that understands you better than you know yourself.

"You know twice in a lifetime is pushing it don't you?"

Well that came out of the middle of nowhere, I now officially had no idea what he was talking about.

"Huh?"

"Being left on my doorstep." He placed a finger thoughtfully on his chin like he was remembering the scene perfectly. "The first time when you were a newborn baby and this time makes twice. Like I said, twice in one lifetime is pushing it..."

I sat up quickly, the wet cloth on my forehead falling into my lap.

"You have to be kidding me? I was left on your doorstep as a baby" I said.

His grin made everything normal again.

"My God you hit your head harder than I thought." He said shaking his head from side to side. "You think I would have put up with all your crap growing up if you were some stray I'd found in a cardboard box?"

"Sure you would..." I said. "I'm lovable, what can I say?"

Letting myself slip back to horizontal, I pulled the cloth back to my forehead, covering my painful eyeballs.

He sat back. If he wasn't still leaning over me that was a good sign. Perhaps I'd escaped being locked up until my twenty first birthday.

My Dad knew me...if I was being challenging I wouldn't be dying anytime soon. I may have kept his Fatherly hormones in control just this once...

"Yeah okay, I would have put up with your crap from the first moment I saw your fat little face, but do you mind telling me how you ended up unconscious on the doorstep of the Bookshop? Are you going to try to tell me you fainted while putting your key in the lock of something because I'm not buying it." A slight tremor in his voice betrayed the fact that he was still nervous and maybe even a little scared for me.

Ah, what a sweetie.

I looked out from under the washcloth really concerned, "I had a fat face?"

Laughing he raised his hand, "Sure you're awake?"

I smirked and reaching out a hand laid it across the back of his, giving it a little squeeze and me time to think and make up my mind.

There was no way I was getting my Father mixed up in this any deeper than he already was. Sure he was a big guy and all, but too much of the last day or so was on the witchy Nana Tottot Sam Ray supernatural side of life and death. Having a skeptical overprotective Father as a bodyguard was a recipe for a big goopy disaster and worse he might actually get hurt.

If this is the place where you scoff and say "Well what about you Sam? Won't you get hurt too?"

The answer is probably in the affirmative but I've grappled with a few challenging situations at Nana's side, not least of which, the last time. I thought with sadness. One day I'll have the time to go into details but right now things are a bit hectic, it will have to wait. Let's just say black magic and its wielders are not a completely new experience for me...

Make no mistake, when it comes to the scary supernatural stuff I have a few tricks up my sleeve. With luck and the wind in the right direction maybe I'll pull them out at the right time, avoid blowing my head of its shoulders and scrape through. Knowledge, skills and confident faith will get you further than muscle, age and a penis. I guarantee it.

"Is it drugs?" he said, his voice low and almost non-existent. "I've read about it. You think it can never happen to your kids and...ouch!"

I have to admit that at this point I was responsible for my Father's 'ouch', I had considered a quick slap upside the head but after all he is my Dad so I made sure I was respectful. With a quick word under my breath and mentally squeezing my temples I sent a quick jolt of electricity through him.

Not entirely the most difficult achievement, the air

is full of minute quantities of electricity, all I did was bundle, bind and direct it towards the closest dumb object that, despite the rubbish he's been speaking, is well grounded. I know. Ironic huh?

"Ouch" he said again, his hair raised in spikes across the top of his head like a small forest of Christmas trees.

Maybe I should really concentrate and add a few strings of lights, there would be enough electricity to create a nice festive scene even if winter had been and gone months ago.

But that was one of the troubles with my power so far...I could divert, tap into, enhance and grab supernatural handfuls of natural forces but as for creating a mechanical or technical object, that was completely beyond what I could achieve.

I've read a little about the power and what I don't know is a gazillion times greater than what I do, but from what Nana taught me and from what I've been able to determine for myself, my power is gained from nature. What nature can do, if I'm disciplined, I can tap into it. That's it put nice and simplistically. Sure there's much more to it than that but that's a good place to start.

I hope this isn't too gross but for the record, my power only truly materialized after my first menstrual cycle. That means I've been able to experiment for the past three years give or take. But growing up around Nana Tottot was like going to the University of Witchcraft and graduating magna cum laude.

I moved quickly on before I got that sick sad feeling again.

So...I have a lot to learn and no one to teach me. Part of wanting to come to Salem was the hope that maybe...just maybe I would meet a person that had ten percent of the power of Nana Tottot. If I could find that person then perhaps I could learn to use the power I felt growing within me every day.

I didn't think it was dangerous or anything... the chances of me going 'Kaboom' without the right tuition was one in a thousand or one in five hundred on a bad day. Reassured? No, me neither.

I glanced at my Father, still rubbing his shin while his hair threatened to poke my eyes out.

"Don't be such a baby" I told him. "And serves you right for being such an idiot. Drugs...I don't take Aspirin, even that causes me problems, there's more chance of you being on drugs than me. Anyway, where were we?"

Now I knew what we had been discussing before I had given him a tiny shock - How I came to be on the same doorstep as the murdered girl, unconscious but thankfully with all eight pints of blood coursing around all of my still attached extremities. But I was hoping the little jolt I'd given him would push our conversation out of his mind.

"If you think that little parlor trick is going to make me forget what we were talking about then you must think I'm senile. So...again, how the hell did you pass out just outside of the shop?" my Father said.

I knew the chances of the electricity working again would get me grounded, so the truth, almost.

"I honestly don't know Dad. Maybe I just fainted from burning the candle at both ends. You know...getting the shop ready. Not eating real well as most of the cooking stuff is still packed..."

"Forgive this nautical term you'll probably not understand but that's bullshit lady. You start opening the door, feel yourself fainting so start hammering the damned door off its hinges to get my attention before you keel over...like I said, that just smelly brown bull crap young lady."

"Oh. Someone knocked?" I asked.

Damned. Bang went that theory. I was brought here.

"Yes someone knocked and thank God they did. If they hadn't you'd probably still be outside, in a pile and with luck all that would have happened to you would be a few dogs emptying their bladders on your unconscious head. It was that crazy knocking that got me to go take a look. So do you want to tell me what's going on?"

I looked at him, the ridges across his forehead,

his tight thin lips, wide open sea blue eyes and my heart melted. I wanted so badly to curl up with his Fatherly arms around me, keeping me warm and safe, making sure the bad guys stayed outside. But I couldn't do it. Maybe I would have three or four years ago, hell, maybe I would have the day before the power arrived. But the day it did everything changed. I was blessed and cursed all at the same time. The day my power came was the day that I had to start putting my arms around others that needed my help, not the other way around.

Biting my lip I shook my head from side to side, trying not to let any tears peek out from the corners of my eyes that were fighting me for airtime. Crying would screw up everything. He needed to understand I was a grown up and if I didn't manage to make him see that now then he would never see it.

This is it Dad. I have to do this on my own. I thought as he took onboard that I was going to refuse his help.

I shook my head.

Something in his face changed just a little, his lips squeezing a little tighter, the corner of his eyes bulging at the corners as he closed them a fraction, trying not to show that I'd hurt him by not falling at his feet and wrapping my arms around his shins.

This was the end of an era. I knew it and so did he. Releasing a breath slowly he sat back, the corners of his mouth turning up in a faint smile, the first clue he was getting it, understanding my need to do this.

It was time for me to stand on my own two feet. Now don't imagine for second that I won't holler like a stuck pig if something that requires a Dad's special talents comes up.

But if there's one conclusion I've come to in the last forty eight hours it's that a witch would be more able to handle the recent events than a retired Navy Commander.

Sorry Mr. President I know you spent a fortune on him but that's just the plain truth. This was my sandbox. Even if I was pretty green and new to the said sandbox.

Sitting up I thought back to the last images I'd experienced before passing out. The boots, the hand reaching out, my scratches. Looking at my nails I knew exactly what I needed to do.

Pushing down on my Father's shoulder I forced myself to stand. I just hoped it wasn't too late.

"Where are you going? You're in no conditi..."

"Just going to my room Dad. Stop stressing okay?"

And just like that I'd escaped the attack of the uptight Father.

Whew, that was close.

Chapter 17

Pushing the door closed I leant against the surface, listening and waiting. Silence. Then after a minute I heard him muttering to himself as he cleared away plates and cups in the kitchen.

That meant he was arguing with himself about what he should have said or done different. He's probably telling himself that he should have been firmer, more fatherly. He's funny.

It was because he knows how to give me space that we hadn't ever really gone for each other's throats. Perhaps it's because we're all each other have. It's always been like that since as long as I can remember.

Standing away from the door, I look around the shambles that I loosely call my room, looking for what I needed until my eyes settled on a black leather Doctor's bag I'd found in a flea market during a trip to New Orleans almost three years ago now.

Sitting down on the bed I lifted it up beside me, it smelt of wax polish and felt good as I ran my fingers across the dimpled black leather, appreciating the way it felt, worn and comfortable, the big leather flap arriving at the brass lock keeping it closed.

Locating the gold chain at the back of my neck, I followed it around to my chest, pulling it out from beneath my shirt, a small brass key.

I leant towards the black Doctor's bag, fit the key in the lock and turned it with a click. The brass lock jumped open allowing me to pull back the leather strap.

Leaning back I held my breath then opened up the bag, always surprised by how the mouth of it was as wide and broad as the bags thick leather walls. I looked inside, mentally cataloguing each plastic bag and container pinned or stacked from one end to the other.

Reaching into one of the hundreds of side pockets I pulled out a stick of plain white chalk and with fingers poised and gently waving above the multitude of items, I saw what I needed. With a click of my tongue on the roof of my mouth I grabbed a small glass beaker with a plastic sealable top. Briefly holding it up to the light I confirmed what I thought – empty.

Reaching into a different side pocket I pulled out a perfectly clean nail file.

Popping off the plastic top I held each of my fingers over the glass beaker running the file under each nail, collecting the fragments.

With each of my fingers done I gave the small pieces a shake watching them rattle around in the bottom of the plastic container before sealing the lid.

Holding my breath I ran the calculations in my head, counting down the hours and minutes from when I passed out until now. It was really close but I still had a shot.

Sitting with my hands around the container I closed my eyes, thinking back through the conversation I'd had with my Father I dragged up the feelings I'd had when I turned away from his help, the look on his face, trembling lips and two tears appeared at the corner of my eyes.

Carefully I brought the container up to each eye, collecting the two tears. Running my thumb around I put the lid back on and moved it around in a circle, the tears coming together with my nail fragments.

Placing the container on the floor, I directed my power with thought, gesture and word. A glow flickered within the container and as I concentrated grew into a burning light. The heart aching loss I felt finally admitting to my Father I was no longer his little girl combined with the fragments of skin and hair I'd scratched from the back of my attacker's hand. Now it was my turn to mutter under my breath, securing the power in my hands.

The light faded somewhat, guttering and calming to a constant. As that light flickered and settled, it leant against one side of the container. I smiled knowing the spell had worked. The loss captured within those tears had reacted with skin under my nails.

Picking up the container I turned it first one way

then the other, feeling some satisfaction the light stayed pointing in one direction. As long as the light glowed I'd be able to find who I scratched.

Letting out a breath I hadn't even realized I'd been holding I felt relief. Despite the amount of time since the scratch, its life force was still powerful enough to work with my spell. The challenge was always keeping the light burning. It would feed on the power I'd added and on the fragments themselves. Given the time that had elapsed since I'd fainted, the light could go out at any moment.

If I was lucky I'd have a few hours and if I was unlucky the light would cease before I left my bedroom... I dragged my gym clothes off and prayed the light would stay bright.

Leather boots, velvet skirt, bodice and crimson lipstick then pinching my cheeks.

Alright Sam time to get out there and take the fight to them. Now all I needed to do was figure out what the hell I was going to do when I found the person I'd scratched, assuming the light lasted that long.

Biting my lip I said a silent prayer that I'd be lucky enough to see the morning. My head throbbed from banging it on the floor and I was about to go walking around the night with a container of light like some modern day Florence Nightingale.

Glancing at my watch it was just after eleven.

The whole night stretched ahead.

Oh Joy. Lucky me.

Chapter 18

The light leaned. I tried not to stare directly at it but that was impossible. It was my compass through the darkness.

I looked away blinking, the night enveloping me. I stretched my eyes wider, trying to see despite my night vision having been burnt away.

Trying not to trip I ran through the streets of Salem, my breath quickening as I picked up the pace. Trying to keep the panic from my thoughts, I hurried along, mindless of much around me.

The flesh and hair I'd put into the container had combined with my tears of loss to point the way to the owner of the scratches. Unfortunately they were also the fuel that kept the light burning.

It had been a tiny amount of skin that I'd scrapped from under my nails, and even now as the light faded, threatening to extinguish itself.

Glancing around I tried to keep my feet moving without stumbling, the last thing I needed was to fall flat on my face and break the container in my ham fisted hands. It would be just like me to do exactly that. Holding it tighter I turned into Hawthorne Boulevard, walking over the place where I'd fainted before.

The upside of running through Salem just past midnight was that there weren't too many people around to watch me acting like a Lunatic. But as I ran there were still a handful of people, but with bloodshot eyes they mostly looked the worse for a few too many drinks. I willed them to forget all about the panting Goth girl running past them holding an unflickering light, closing my eyes briefly as I pushed out a strong blank thought, and followed with a slight finger gesture.

Luck, a little mind nudge and a body full of beer would make me a figment of their subconscious when tomorrow rolled around. By the time their Alka-Seltzer dissolved they'd have forgotten all about me. Fingers crossed.

Pulling back my thoughts I blinked my eyes open and gasped dodging a completely still trash can sneaking up on me when I was playing with the locals. You have to watch those trash cans. Thank goodness I'm not a klutz!

Watching it retreat over my shoulder, I jumped to the side as a street light jumped out while I was watching the can. What is this? A conspiracy? Or me nearly walking into inanimate objects? Don't answer that.

Holding the light forward I cheered at having survived the street furniture obstacle course.

I tripped.

Falling to the sidewalk, my knee lost the argument with the sharp edged tiles of the pathway, a nice slice also taken out of my hand as it shot forward automatically trying break my fall, the other wanting to forget the container and land palm out.

With a stifled scream I saw my fingers loosen.

With a determined 'No' I fought my own mind, tightening instead of loosening my fingers, letting myself fall forward without protection.

Despite my mind threatening me I kept my hands around the guiding light as my knees lost their battle with the sidewalk. The deep graze making my jaw clamp down stifling a yell.

Dammit, what was I thinking? Tell the world you're not a klutz and the world will always have the last laugh. Guaranteed.

The pain causing my vision to spot I took a deep steadying breath.

Picturing a smooth empty box, I took the pain and shoved it inside, closing the lid with a snap. I opened my eyes.

All I saw was my guiding light failing, little more than a glowing matchstick head. Gritting my teeth I stood and willed my feet to pick up the pace in a semi-panic.

I was running up Hawthorne Boulevard towards Salem Common at midnight.

Great. Just great. Just what a seventeen year old

girl shouldn't be doing... running around a barely lit park in the middle of the night.

My Father would be pleased.

How about we keep this one between us okay?

At the corner of Hawthorne my hand rested on the iron fence surrounding the common. Light from the road side fought with the shadows of the unlit park and won the first twenty feet. After, the light began to feather and fragment, patches of blackness taunted with their impenetrability. Say what you like, once the filament of an electric light bulb warms up it really does throw off a good curtain of light, thanks for everything Thomas.

I could tell that light stretched around the edges but deep in the middle there was a pool of concentrated shadow untouched every night for centuries.

On the edge of Salem Common, sweating from the pace despite a breeze, the guiding light pointing in one constant direction, the heart of the darkness.

The light flickered, then did the unthinkable, leaning one way then the other. I realized it was following the owner of the scratches.

Okay you say, so it's following the owner of the scratches...no biggie right?

Wrong. This light was jumping side to side way too fast. If it was following the scratches then either my spell was screwed up or...

Actually I didn't have any other explanation. My spell must be screwed up, people don't move as fast as the light was flickering.

They just don't.

Period.

Saying every curse word I could think of, I stepped off the curb and walked through the circle of light into Salem's night time forest. As I walked into the cold I considered perhaps this is one of those times when the heroine, one Sam Ray, should have stayed on the path to grandma's house instead of venturing off.

The back of my neck prickled like a hand was poised waiting to grab, shake and tell me I was being the biggest idiot in Massachusetts.

Hell why limit it to just one state.

Believe me, if I thought I had a choice I wouldn't be here, I could have stayed at the Bookshop, tucked up nice and warm in my split personality futon. The lightened to find out who I scratched was forcing me to go bad use of language, re-write –into the center of the common, the darkest place in Salem.

I'm pretty proud of my curses. They've taken me years of collecting and practice but I've had the best teachers, Nana Tottot and dear old Dad. Dad you say? I'm not taking about calling forth clouds of locusts or swarms of frogs, I'm talking about the 'Son of a Sea horse's ass' type curses. And walking into the dark stimulated some choice curse words insisting I heard them out loud as I take each step forward.

Sorry folks but when fear is threatening to make my breakfast lunch and dinner smother the grey daisies at my feet, sometimes turning the air blue with swear words helps me keep the bodily fluids where they're supposed to be.

In this case I referenced a Baboon's ass or for those that don't know it's a Navy reference to corned beef. Not my best curse, but I'm just warming up.

The light followed the owner of the scratches still dancing and flickering faster than a person can travel and I had no explanation.

Trying to picture what could move back and forth silently in the dark that fast made my head swim. It's crazy to walk into the Common at midnight, it's certifiable to do it knowing the person who attacked you is able to move at impossible speeds, silently.

What the hell was I dealing with? And why was I still here and not in Acapulco with a fruit punch and an umbrella? Was it courage or stupidity? Yeah, I know. Both.

Five pathways spread out dividing the common into even slices of night.

Each path tempted me. Maybe one taken would have different consequences than another, one to safety, another taking me into the closing jaws of the devil himself? How was I to choose?

Persuading myself it was just the night getting colder, I failed to resist a shiver which spasmed my body making my teeth clack together.

I waited, unsure. The light pointed, demanding. Loud in my ears.

Chapter 19

Taking the middle pathway. My feet moved of their own accord, hands cupping the dwindling light. As I watched it guttered, disappeared for a second then sputtered to slight life.

Stepping way beyond the street light halo, relying upon the weak light in my hands. It was all I had.

My body responded pumping adrenaline throughout my body,

I took a deep breath consciously making a focused effort to calm myself down. Swallowing I felt a little better and looked around.

A war memorial to my left, four columns encircled by chain, threadbare American flags lifeless in the stale night. Walking past I could smell urine, and for found myself wondering who could disrespect a place like this by pissing on it. Shaking my head I moved on.

Suddenly the flame within my hands jumped, bursting out from between my fingers. The light fell, it was out before it even hit the ground.

I was left alone blind, with empty hands, smelling urine and amazed that it wasn't my own.

Standing still I squeezed my eyes shut waiting until they grew accustomed to the night, my hands clasped together as I reached out with my other senses. I felt alone and that was just fine with me...better to be alone than sense someone was close.

A dog screamed, shocking me to my toes, my feet readying to run. I violently turn right then left, needing to find the origin of the ghastly sound, my imagination working overtime. Images of a dog with a bloody cut throat, opened by some midnight fiend, the same that tore apart the girl.

"Dammit, what the hell..." I said needing to hear my own voice. Summoning a slither of courage I took a step piercing the barrier of fear holding me back, I began to walk.

My tentative half steps lengthened, willing whatever was ahead to try and do its worst. Tightening my jaw I realized something. I'd rather fight and die than live hiding in fear. Having made that decision I felt better, I was in it up to my neck and felt good about myself no matter where this ended.

Striding forward my foot almost missed a beat as the sounds of a scuffle came out from ahead. Trying to pick apart the noises I heard what sounded like feet and claws scrapping across stone and overlain with a mixture of grunts, groans, striking and a rattling choke I've never heard before.

My need to discover overcame my fear. Running forward an ancient small domed building appeared ahead. It was a pretty architectural contribution to the park, probably used in the summer innocently as a band stand with children playing on the grass beneath. In contrast two bodies too far away for features grabbed and flailed at each other on the domes raised platform. Falling down together, one on top of the other, the uppermost struck over and over.

"Stop, stop" I shouted running closer breathless from panic as I strained to see, my mind trying to make sense of the night shaded jigsaw puzzle of taupe and black.

Breath rasping I ran, arriving at steps leading to the platform where the bodies were still clasped together, jumping forward, I took them two at a time. At the top my feet almost slipped out from under me hitting a wet slickness. Throwing a hand the top of an iron railing, steadying myself.

A dark mass writhed less than ten steps away. Trying to distinguish features I moved closer. I heard tearing, snuffling and blowing as if through clogged nostrils, and what sounded like bones being pulled upon and snapped like a giant turkey wishbone.

Then a near overwhelming smell of blood, made me gag even as my stupidly courageous feet inched me closer forward. My eyes slowly grew accustomed to the lack of light under the stone gazebo as my feet stole away the distance between me and the writhing shapes.

They came together like a slap as a bloody snout turned away from the bloody body it was buried up to its claws in, as it first smelt me, then saw me.

It was enormous. A wolf or, taking a crazy step forward, a man wolf or a creature somewhere between a wolf and a Gorilla. Wolves have an inherent beauty but there was nothing beautiful about this. It was made for one purpose only, to kill.

The beast was a ghastly collection of tufts of black sprouting coarse hair from thickened elephantine skin, claws and teeth. Teeth beside yet more teeth. It crouched down over a girl's body as she gurgled her last breath.

Remember what I was saying about better to fight and all that jazz? All said before I met this eating machine.

My legs started to move even before my brain caught up, getting a head start while my synapses took their sweet time putting all the facts together. My left and right leg knew what they were doing, knowing my brain would agree when it finally unfroze itself and processed the data...all those teeth, plus man sized Gorilla-come-wolf, plus dead guy equals run the hell in the opposite direction arms pumping. My legs knew my brain would agree when it started functioning again and if it didn't well tough luck, at least it would still be alive to be pissed and it could damn well be more appreciative. 'Ass' was silent between both camps, happy someone was saving it.

Time to get the hell out of here.

With a twist my legs turned and ran, with another less graceful twist my right ankle went in the opposite direction as it slid across the bloody floor. Reaching for the iron railing, I choked on a scream as my fingertips brushed against the cold metal without managing to get a firm hold.

I missed it. My legs slid out from underneath me.

Faster than you can say 'twisted ankle' white pain was exploding in my head.

Not hesitating I started dragging my ass towards the stairs. The creature turned, its tooth filled mouth seemed to smile as it disengaged from the body, looking almost sad at the prospect of leaving his dinner.

As it put one clawed foot in front of the other, brain joined the party noting the strangest things. Its two front arms looked less like a wolves than the arms of a steroid enhanced power-lifter, the rear legs like a powerful gazelle's.

Lowering its head it skittered forward on taloned claws, not functioning too efficiently on the smooth tiles. I could smell its blood encrusted fur, its panting mouth, jaundiced eyes met mine and seeing some recognition I gambled.

Reaching out a hand, hoping it would stay attached, I said the one word which I hoped would save my life.

"Raul"

Chapter 20

If claws have an index finger then his was reaching out towards me, a long nail dirty with mud and blood.

I sat as still as I could, my hand outstretched, not knowing if any additional movement would be the trigger that would turn this slow moving animal into a slicing dicing claw liquidizer.

The nail moved closer, veined and curved. My breath froze as the nail reached me, stretching until, stopping, it moved the hair from my eye.

Opening its tooth ridden mouth, a crooning exuded from the depths of its rippled rubbery neck. As it was partly human I saw expressions I couldn't explain, like it was ashamed.

Enough Dammit! Without any real plan I took hold of his thick wrist, my fingers not completely encircling the bone and gristle of his limb.

He took a deep breath, a talon poised stationary in front of my face, staying perfectly still. Was he toying with me? This could just be a sick prelude before striking his claws down my chest, before forcefully tearing my life from my flesh.

Trying to suppress the fear which washing over me, I brushed my fingers across his skin. It was thick and hot to the touch, certainly much warmer than humans.

"Raul. Is that you?"

His mouth opened wider, letting out a whimper, trying to talk from a mouth not designed for it. Snatching his hand away he balanced on the balls of his feet, his long snout snuffling and snapping in each direction – was he readying to tear me apart or flee?

With a growl his powerful hands slapped the ground. Leaping from one side of the hexagonal platform, clearing the ruptured body, blood pooling all around.

Sliding against the cold iron fence the body between us, the werewolf crouched, its head and tongue lolling, powerful arms encircling its knees.

I stood without the faintest idea what to do next. Should I get out while the getting was good? Looking down at the body the thought of lying and dying beside the girl already there was scary as all hell.

You may think you've excepted that one day you'll die, but you can't truly excepted it until you've had death smile at you, its teeth deadly and beautiful. Taking a breath of the freshest air I appreciated the few seconds I was being given, the slight reprieve I'd won. The smell of the blood was strong, but even that was enhanced as I stood in the near silence of the night, crickets chirping telling me the world hadn't gone completely comic book.

But I was lying on the floor, hand outstretched onto the bottom rungs of an iron fence, feet splayed out having lost my footing in a pool of blood.

Directly across, a Werewolf crouched, powerful arms wrapped around its knees pulled up to its chest, its head hidden between its knees.

Between me and it, a dead body.

Peering into the darkness I strained to make out the girl.

Like mine, her legs were splayed, but her shoes pointed in opposite directions, nylon legs covered in sticky crimson, a skirt which had ridden up to the triangle crotch of the pantyhose.

Looking past her lower body, was a gapping jacket and shirt, a dark purple hole offering me a view straight into the girl's chest, two small breasts to be separated forever by ribs pulled up and outwards to reveal a twitching heart.

Not sure how I'd ever look at anything again, my eyes continued up.

Strangely and perhaps mercifully the girl's face was completely untouched, she looked relaxed, asleep, strawberry red hair framing a delicate boned face, pretty enough to be a Disney character.

But no Prince Charming would revive this girl with

a loving kiss, not unless he had a spare heart packed in ice and could be here in the next seventeen seconds or so.

Still looking at her face I gagged as I noticed her lips were moving,

"She's still alive." I heard my disconnected voice saying, "My Gods she's still alive..."

Pulling myself towards her across the bloody floor I put my hands across the broad hole in her chest even though I knew it wouldn't do any good. I still felt like it would help in some way, perhaps it was just about having contact with her, or protecting the heart... I was acting rationally but it seemed like the right thing to do.

Turning my face sideways, I put my ear close to her barely moving lips expecting to hear a prayer, perhaps some entreaty to me or her God not to let her die. I sobbed. I knew such a wish would be like throwing a quarter in the mall fountain.

But there were no prayers, no pleading for life. She said one thing before she coughed, took a last rattling breath and died.

"The wolf..."

Chapter 21

I closed my eyes as she did, she for the last time, me because I felt heart sick, her fragile life passing me by as it left her body. My power comes from nature. One of the downsides is sensing when death come and pulls life out by the roots, releasing it so it can go wherever spirits journey after they leave the shell of their body, broken and still.

The girl's essence passed me by and turned my head towards the wolf, crouching in the shadows. As I watched I heard what sounded like a half growl, half sob and saw it shaking. Not able to pull my eyes away, the wolf began to change, and the sounds of grief replaced by the grunting of excruciating pain. Bones cracked as the body shifted and seemed to reorganize itself right in front of me.

The werewolf broke like a giant's invisible hand was remolding a flesh and blood with no consideration for what was possible or painful. It stretched, twisted, broke and jammed together elements of the beast, into what was beginning to resemble a human form.

The transformation looked tortuous, the pain to break and reset every bone would be maddening to any entity.

The process slowed, my nose twitched with the heavy, pungent smell of sweat and moist leather.

I thought about trying to stand on my twisted ankle as the werewolf changed. If there was a time when the beast should be vulnerable this was it. But I just couldn't do it.

Not because of any weakness in me but because I couldn't face leaving the girl alone, even in death, even it meant my own. She deserved to be treated with more respect. Being found in the early morning by some passing stranger after a night being picked at by night animals was unthinkable.

Making up my mind I held onto the girl's hand and

watched the transformation until all that was left was a squatting naked man, his face still hidden between his knees. There was blood on the soles of feet, the tops and soles two different shades of tan. His hands, had elongated fingers even though his nails had retracted, dissolved or whatever the hell they do when he changes back.

His body still shook but the growl had been replaced by wracking spasms passing through his whole body, despite the reddened hands that pulled his knees up tight.

"What the hell did you do?" I heard myself saying.

The night was completely quiet, as if waiting, listening, to understand how a fragile beauty could have experienced such violence.

His sobbing increased, his head shielded from view.

"Hey. Answer me you son of a bitch. How could you? Look at her you bastard. Look at what you did."

He looked up at me, snot running down his face ignored, blood splatters freckling his cheeks and forehead. Eyes embedded in his red smeared Halloween face, looked out at me weeping. He tried to blink away the tears looking across the girl's violently fractured body.

Across the back of his blood smeared hand, an angry red scratch.

It was Raul.

He shook his head, over and over, moving vigorously as the echoes of my accusations bounced and died between the stone columns of dome.

Still shaking his head he rocked backwards and forward like an addict in withdrawal.

Then, licking his lips as he struggled to form words.

"No...No...No...No. It wasn't...I..."

"What? Wasn't you? You didn't just nearly rip this girl's heart out from her chest? You expect me to believe you? I just saw you. Up to your elbows in her chest. You Raul. No one else. Just you..."

"But..."

His sentence broke into a howl of sheer pain and confusion. Before I could say anything else he jumped up and vaulted off the platform onto the grass of Salem's Common beneath. Sprinting off it took less than four strides until he disappeared into the darkness.

Left alone with the dead girl.

Now that Raul, the werewolf or whatever the hell he was had left I could look at her properly. It hit me hard as I committed her face and features to memory.

She was a near mirror image of the girl killed outside the Bookshop of Horror. She looked just like me.

Chapter 22

The strobing light, yellow tape and the drying blood were all that was left as the ambulance pulled away, the girl's body lifted silently into its gapping mouth by green faced ambulance drivers moments before.

Perhaps it was respect or the fact her cadaver had all eternity but it left, it's light and sirens at peace, the sun dazzled me with my first glimpse of a new day.

I took a deep and shaky breath, feeling the cold of an early morning fill my lungs, a cloud exhaling from my mouth.

My appreciation of basically everything was disturbed by a person clearing their throat, looking to be noticed. I tried to pull my eyes away from the huge picnic blanket sized smear of blood where she had been. It looked like some kind of warped art work, long lines etched across where my feet had slipped, bigger than possible paw prints. Boot imprints from coroners after the police had finished. The shapes of slipping a sliding meshed together telling their own story in the center of the platform, the space still for the first time in hours, except for the crime tape vibrating in the breeze with a strum.

I allowed myself to be pulled away, a strong hand turning me around.

Officer Trublood looked me over, but not for cuts and bruises, he was interested in what my eyes told him, weighing up how far gone I was. Damn close to the edge, but I wasn't going to tell him that.

I wanted to reassure him, to tell him I was going to be okay, fine, that I could deal with this. But I couldn't. I wasn't. I felt wretched, sick and scared. How do you get over images like that? It's not some television show that you can turn off when it scares the crap out of you. I'd love to change the channel, to leave the bedside light before going to sleep. Anything so I don't wake up in the middle of the night in a cold heart beating sweat, I'd try them all. But they wouldn't be enough.

Werewolves exist.

They actually truly exit for God's sake...

And one of them was killing girl's that looked a hell of a lot like me and if that wasn't enough, I couldn't convince myself that I wasn't going to be next...each victim had been killed just steps away from me and I had watched them as they took their last breath.

I was at the center of all this and it was real.

I had stumbled upon each murder. Seeing their last seconds without seeing the death cut.

Why hadn't he done to me what he'd done to the girl? He could have pulled my throat out faster than a child snatches at candy. He could have slowly and deliberately torn me apart, piece by piece –Instead he reached out to me.

I wouldn't bet my beating heart on it but my senses told me he had a soul that was lonely and alone. With that thought rattling around I did exactly that – I bet my heart on it.

"Officer Trublood. Is this your crime scene or were you just passing on your morning jog?"

He smiled, his teeth reminding me of Raul for a small instant. I don't think I would ever see a smile right again.

"You know for a girl that's just seen her second murder in so many days – you've got an interesting way about you Ms. Ray..."

"Interesting how Officer?"

His fingers pulled absentmindedly at the yellow crime tape, before he looked up at me.

"You do understand they look a hell of a lot like you but without the Goth? And you're the lucky girl who keeps finding the bodies. If I was a suspicious man..." his sentence hanging between us.

I felt my ears growing red, my fingers grasping at my side as I considered tearing a throat out too.

"You have got to be kidding me? I'm running around in the middle of the night dressed as a wolf, cutting up girls who look like me? What? You think maybe I'm taking out all the cute red heads in Salem? Maybe I can't stand the competition is that it?" through clenched teeth, my hands twitching.

Giving me the Trublood "shit kicking" smile he stood in silence then with oil in his voice he said.

"Dressed as a Wolf Ms. Ray?"

Shit. "Right – I've had enough."

Walking down the steps and finally away from the crime scene. Trying to stamp dramatically down the steps, my weakened ankle gave way. Trublood's hand caught me, walking me down each step to the grass below.

"Look, I'm sorry okay." He said contrite, "that was a stupid thing to say. I don't think you are on a murdering spree but you are running around in the middle of the night and seem to turn up just as these crimes happen. I should have someone follow you just so we can be there for the next one." Looking at him in shock, he considered it then shaking his head continued, "...somehow you are connected to this Ms. Ray."

"You're right." I said pulling my arm hard from his grip.

Trublood's head jerked around, his eyes focused on nothing but me.

"I am?"

"Yes...Definitely. That was a stupid thing to say."

A little of the arrogance left him, his chest just a little less inflated.

I went on with a little more sympathy for him.

"Look, don't you think all of this has crossed my mind? You don't think I've realized the murderer is killing a certain type? You need to look for a wolf and as I gave up fluffy animals on my eighth birthday, I can't help you." I said.

"You saw a wolf attacking the girl?"

I thought about the question then shrugged.

"I'm not a hundred percent sure what I saw. It could have been a wolf, but until I ran up those steps they were just lumps in the darkness and then..."

Trublood's lips pulled tight.

"...and then?", he said taking a hold of my elbow, doing his best to offer some support.

"Then I thought I saw a wolf but the girl had already been torn apart. Her chest was gapping."

"So you didn't see it happen?"

"No." I said quietly. "I didn't".

"But it was a wolf?" he asked, too much in my space.

I paused.

Desperate to tell him everything but I Nana told me to trust in my instincts, I couldn't.

It came down to this moment. If I could slap myself upside the head for being more stupid than I could remember without looking like a freak, I'd do it right now.

"Yes...it was...a wolf", my voice little more than a breath.

Trublood stared intently at me, chewing on his bottom lip. Making up his mind he began to turn away, then stopped, looking back at me.

"A wolf Ms. Ray?"

I felt like there was a sword poised above my head, such a short and simple question but with fatal consequences if I answered poorly. At the top of the list of potential victims, my name.

I made up my mind.

"Didn't you see the prints around the body?

Trublood didn't take his eyes off me.

"We saw the paw prints but you know what's funny?"

My heart started beating faster, he wanted me to ask but I was strong, I could resist.

"Funny?" I asked quickly.

"Yes. The body was surrounded by paw prints in the blood. The creature just about danced with the girl as she bled to death, its prints were everywhere..."

"So?" I said, my fingers giving an axe earrings a twist.

"So? That much blood you'd expect the prints would lead away from the scene wouldn't you? Perhaps down the steps? At the very least in the grass surrounding the gazebo. But you know what?"

There was no way I was going to keep being a player in Trublood's little pantomime. No way at all.

"No paw prints?" I said as I tried to bite my tongue.

He smiled, think cat eating canary..."No paw prints. But there were a few human foot prints and they had no shoes." He said. "Can you imagine that? Sized nine feet and no shoes. Don't you think that's funny?"

If that sword I'd imagined had have been real it would just have taken my head off and Officer Trublood would have his hands firmly around the handle. He knew I was not telling the whole truth and all he needed to do now was fill in the blanks.

Give him a few late nights, and some lucky breaks and he'd have all the answers. I had no doubt about it. And when he did, I'd been in deep brown stuff.

Normally it would bother me but as I was walking under the threat of being dismembered by Raul the psycho skate wolf, I'd cross the Trublood crisis when I came to it.

"What was the question again Officer?" I asked.

"I said – Don't you think that's funny given you saw a wolf and just a wolf? You know if you think you were mistaken you can tell me. It happens all the time when people have experienced something as traumatic as a murder...Twice."

"I saw a wolf, tripped and twisted my ankle. After that I was on the floor next to the dead girl. All I could see was her. Nothing else was more important than her. You understand?" a pleading tone to my voice.

He froze for a moment then nodded. "Yeah, I think I do Ms. Ray. Thanks for your help. Hopefully it will help us catch this guy before he does it again. But you know what?"

I gave in for the last time. Answering him as tiredness washed over me.

"What Officer?"

"The time between murders in these kinds of

cases gets shorter the more people they kill. We've had...what? Twenty four hours give or take between these two murders?"

"Twenty four hours" I whispered as I started the long walk back across the Common, picking up my light container on my way back to the Bookshop of Horror. Fifteen minutes of zombie like shuffling and I'd let myself into the bookshop, groaning as I passed the half empty boxes of books still to stack

Two minutes later I was under the covers, fully clothed, feeling I'd wasted too much time as it was unzipping and pulling off my muddy leather boots.

I closed my eyes and...

Chapter 23

My bed was not breathing in time with me.

I lay still.

Kept my eyes closed, convincing myself it was all in my head. I was in bed, at home. Safe and sound.

My bed was breathing.

Maybe I was still dreaming.

When I wake up, my bed won't be breathing and I'll be all alone. Safe, my covers up to my chin.

Trying not to disturb them, I sent my hand sliding slowly and constantly towards my leg.

I never seemed to reach it.

Did I even have legs in this dream?

A leg. Fingers touched.

Crap, I was still wearing my thick velvet skirt. It was doubtful a pinch would wake me through this much material. I know...

I held my breath.

To fool my bed.

It wouldn't know I was going to hold my breath.

With my breath held I heard it.

Breathing.

The futon creaked as someone moved.

I was next. Shit, this was it.

Swallowing all the moisture that had suddenly appeared in my mouth I remembered Nana Tobbot as we'd walk through the burial grounds in Guam.

Laying perfectly still I concentrated, picturing my lungs, my heart, blood flowing and carrying my essence through every fiber of my body. Gaining an appreciation of my center I felt a sense of balance returning.

With a thought, an imagined gesture and silent word I pushed out my awareness and creating a ring of awareness around myself. At first it was tight against my skin but then expanding, reaching out to the person next to me.

Chapter 24

I gasped, images flashing through my mind, a white heat threatening to burn me to dust as my metabolism accelerated, body organs screaming.

Gritting my teeth through the pain I focused on the images, my need to understand greater than any fear. Six girls, all alike.

A baby. A family surrounding it. Smiles, kisses, hugs and then blood and tears.

Images changed, moved to black and white. Flashing through my head faster, like sketches on the corner of a book being flicked to create a childish cartoon.

Running, panting, capture, tearing, blood spray – repeated and repeated and all the while, as the pictures played out I felt– cravings, excitement, satisfaction and finally satiation. I could feel the natural glory of it, the thrill, the excitement and the addiction. But there was no fury or malevolence. It was a hunt but it was a testament to life, to nature, having a place in the order.

Swallowing my fear, I sat up, my bedclothes falling away. Raul looked away, his hands dangling, his shoulders and head slumped, his hair greasy and unwashed.

"It wasn't you." I said quietly.

Raul's shoulders began to shake, his head slumping further, tears pattered on the wooden floor before being wiped away by a dirty and embarrassed foot, black clay under overlong nails.

"Not one memory had you killing anything human. To you being alive is about the wind flowing over your slick fur, your heart pounding as your blood rushes through you...I could feel that in you. No, I could see it."

His head nodded almost imperceptibly. His crying became ragged and snuffling as he managed to get himself under control.

"You know what I said about you not being a

murderer? I lied." He flinched then spun, meeting my eyes for the first time.

"Yeah. I lied. Because I'd sure as hell hate being a rabbit after you've turned."

Raul couldn't help himself. He smiled. Then, in relief than because it was funny, he laughed.

"I breed them..."

"You've got to be kidding me". I said laughing. "You can't even hunt right? You breed them, let them free and run around after them? Damn. What happened to Wolf against prey? Running through the forest at midnight? Freedom?"

I put my hand on his shoulder and squeezed, smiling.

After tapping into his memories, and experiences, I knew what he was and more importantly, what he wasn't.

He wasn't a monster and hadn't killed those girls.

He was different. Like me.

"The wood at midnight...wolf against rabbit..." Raul said.

"Let me guess...Salem Common?"

"He smiled.

"That's why you were there? You were running with the rabbits?"

"Yeah but the girl arrived. Just sort of appeared one minute I had the place to myself, the next she was walking along the path, didn't seem to notice me which sort of freaked me out. How could she miss me, you know?"

I stood up, looking at my bedroom window half open, the lock bent, Raul must have applied some serious pressure to the metal frame from outside.

"Salem Common at night is your place right?" I asked.

He stood, adjusting his beanie, pulling it tighter at the back and straightening it.

"Twice a month for the past year at least."

"You don't take precautions against visitors? Someone wandering across the Common and seeing you in your all over one piece fur coat?"

He looked surprised, the fear and challenges of the last twelve hours dropping away as his common sense returned.

"There's no need. I can hear a squirrel fart from half a mile away. There's no way a girl can wander up and surprise me. I'd hear her first step flattening the grass on the edge of the common. It's happened before. I've always had plenty of time to change back, get dressed and take off before they saw me. And changing isn't a slow process."

Looking at my bedroom window again, he grimaced in apology closed it and pushed hard, bending the lock back into place.

I shrugged like it didn't matter, "But it happened this time. Not only didn't you hear her but she just about walked up and tweaked your nose before you saw her. And weirder still, she ignored the damn big man wolf standing in front of her and did what exactly?"

He thought for a second.

"Went up the steps of the stone gazebo."

"And then?"

"I...I...I don't know."

I stared at him, eyes widening like he was truly afraid.

"What's that supposed to mean? You couldn't see? It was too dark? What?" I asked, my voice urgent.

He scoffed, "You know what I am. You think I can't see a girl standing up on a platform from twenty feet away? It wouldn't matter if it was midnight or a completely moonless night. I mean I don't know..."

"Well..." I interrupted. "What the hell do you know?"

He looked into my face, letting me see him properly for the first time, freckles of blood spattered across his cheeks and forehead.

"That's just it Sam. There's nothing between seeing that girl turn and walk up the stairs and you, falling and twisting your ankle. I thought you were in my imagination. A dream. One minute I was running free and alone, then, without warning, she appeared and was dying at my feet, her hot blood on my hands, across my face. The smell of it a perfume."

His eyes glazing, remembering and as he stood I watched his chest expanding, with a skin creaking sound, thin points at the end of his fingertips, the bone above his lip oscillating like worms writhing beneath the skin, his whole body damp with sweat.

Getting a sick feeling realizing Raul hadn't knowingly killed anyone, but what about unknowingly?

My heart began to pound as I saw and smelt what happening. He was changing and there were no little rabbits to chase in my bedroom.

Chapter 25

"Raul."

He didn't answer.

"Raul..." I said louder.

Shit. There were two of us here but only one of us consciously on planet earth.

Well there was no way I was going to be any one's breakfast, not unless we'd had quite a few dates and had taken the relationship to the next level.

"Raul?" I said my instincts screaming I take the next plane to Guam.

"Raul. Oh shit."

His face. The bones began to shift and gyrate, a growl escaping between his lips. I did the only thing I could think of in the circumstances.

Pulling my hand back I slapped him harder than I've ever hit anything in my entire life.

Raul flew. Rolling beneath my futon.

A snarl came from under it, muffled.

He sat up, wobbling his jaw, a red mark already appearing, shaking his head to get his senses back.

"What was that for?" his tongue tenderly touching the spot where I'd hit him in the corner of his mouth. A spot of blood.

"You were changing. Right here and I couldn't get through to you."

He looked up sharply, his hand falling into his lap.

"What the hell's happening to me Sam? I'm blanking out. And when I do...I don't know..."

I didn't know either but I did know I wanted him out of here. I'd worry about helping him after I knew for sure I wasn't the appetizer on today's specials.

"You need to go somewhere without people Raul. Until we understand what's happening. Is there somewhere you can go?"

Raul thought for a moment, dusting himself down.

"Yeah. Salem Acres. I hunt there sometimes. You'll help me?"

I opened my bedroom door, walking out without answering, having an argument with both my Father and Nana in my head as Raul followed, each taking opposite viewpoints as always.

"You come into my house unannounced and without an invite again and I'll..." I said unlocking the door through to the bookshop.

"Right" he said solemnly. "So you're going to help me?"

In the middle of the bookshop, standing between the boxes I stopped. Raul tugging the strings of his hoodie, nervous, waiting.

I nodded. "Yeah, I'm going to help you. How do I find you at the Acres?"

The lines in his forehead visibly eased, walking past me to the door "The squirrel in the words remember? You need me come to the Acres and call out. I'll be there before you can say Kentucky Fried Chicken..."

I gave him my best wane smile.

"That's great Raul. Let's just make sure I'm not the side order shall we?"

Raul grinned, his teeth perfectly white and sharp.

"You'll never be anyone's side order Sam...Main course maybe..." With a laugh he closed the door, leaving me to my dusty bookshop and my stacks of books.

Chapter 26

Forty minutes later a new, showered, refreshed me was grabbing some toast and making my way out. Running my fingers through my damp hair I looked down at my usual clothes, the boots, skirt, bodice and rings. Being an individual was necessary, part of me but life was getting complicated, loose clothing would slow me down at just the wrong time.

Chewing my lip I made a decision.

A minute later I was in my bedroom, head inside my trunk until I found what I'd been looking for, tugging, it wouldn't give. Pulling harder, planting my feet, with a grunt the pile released it.

With a smile I held up my prize, admiring it as I gave it a shake, easing out the creases it had gained traveling from Guam.

"Just what the Doctor ordered." throwing the outfit onto my bed and running my hands together.

A minute later I was zipping from knee to neck. Looking at myself in the mirror I smiled, appreciating the look. The only way you can get around in Guam is on your own steam. My sixteenth birthday came with a motorbike, I'd insisted, and after much hunting I'd found this little number. I was wearing my own one piece all leather motorcycle suit. Every time I put it on it made me smile, a full suit of black leather that I had to buy after it scared the Bee-Jesus out of me when I'd turned a corner and seen it from the corner of my eye in the bike store window. It kind of reminded me of the Borg out of Star Trek. It was fun and better, I knew it would flatter a girl.

If the going got tough, the thick leather, shoulder and elbow pads would protect me and I looked kick ass.

A great combo, what more could a girl with want?

Nodding at myself in the mirror, I picked up a bag with a few bits and pieces that might come in useful. If all went well it would just be an annoying backpack. If they didn't it would be the nicest backpack on the planet.

Striding through the towers of books, my very own book skyline started to play on my conscience. I'd promised my Father I'd sort this place out. I also sort of promised Raul I'd help. Dammit.

Leaving the bookshop I jumped down the few stairs to the sidewalk and pulled in a deep breath.

Alright Sam, there'd be enough time to stop and smell the coffee later. I knew where I needed to go as soon as Raul had left. Striding back the way I'd ran earlier I wondered how could I have gotten myself into this mess. I'd been in Salem what...two weeks?

With a jangling sense of déjà vu I stood on the edge of Salem Common, it was amazing how different a place can feel when the face of the sun is smiling on it. Last night there were few places as creepy, this morning, the grass couldn't be greener and fresher, if a bunny rabbit sat up and thumped its foot I'd swear Bambi would be along any moment. I couldn't have felt less on the right track. Instinct Sam, instinct.

I hesitated but then saw a father throwing a yellow ring Frisbee to his blond daughter who couldn't have smiled any wider – I felt ridiculous hesitating.

Stepping onto the grass I felt like an interloper, as if I were bringing the darkness of Salem Common night and tainting the purer, happier Salem Common day.

Choosing the same path, a stale urine smell and the memorial appeared and after far fewer steps than last night I came within sight of the stone hexagonal dome, remnants of yellow crime tape fluttering in the happy day breeze. The urine and crime tape reassuring me, if there was a stain on the day, I wasn't the one bringing it.

Taking the steps slowly, wincing as my tender ankle threatened to give out with the occasional twinge. Standing at top of the steps, I would have given just about anything not to touch the yellow tape. I balanced on the edge of the top step, balanced on my toes.

Passing my fingers through my short black hair I dropped my fingers to the zipper of the one piece leather suit, lowering it and fanning myself uselessly with a small pink hand.

I did what I came here for, closing my eyes. I lowered my mental defenses, just as I had after the last murder.

I deconstructed the barriers I kept up at all times , visualizing the child building blocks I used to protect my mind, as I did, found myself whispering a traditional Guam prayer.

It ended by asking forgiveness to the taotaomo'nas – the spirits, as I prepared to walk over the threshold of the stone gazebo, to stand where the girl had been murdered. In Guam if you're smart you ask the spirits before stepping onto a burial ground or a place of death.

I'm not sure why I felt the need to ask the spirits before moving across the crime tape but an echo in the back of my mind demanded it without explaining why, perhaps my subconscious knew more than my conscious mind. The worst that could happen was I spend a minute giving respect to any spirits that may be floating around. Given what I've been through this past few days, I need all the help I can get.

Finishing the prayer I let my eyes open, blinking as the bright sunlight startled for an instant.

Whatever CSI folks do I guessed they'd finished, otherwise guys in white lab coats would still be here on the hands and knees in the dust and blood. What could it hurt me having a look around?

The Gazebo was empty aside from me, the tape and the crusted pool of blood. Even in the short period of time since her death, her life blood had already blackened, beginning to fade and flake. Another day and there would be little sign of her passing, tears came unbidden.

Rubbing them away sniffing I felt a piece of me click inside, swallowing I set my jaw, I was going to do what I could to capture her killer. If it was Raul then I'd put the cuffs on myself and would be at the front of the queue to throw away the key.

Lifting up the tape I ducked down without

breaking it. Perhaps the cops would go easy on me if they came by. Sure.

Standing in the center of the hexagonal platform I ran my fingers through my hair, closing my eyes making ready to drop last of my minds defenses – and even as I visualized the last row of child's blocks, preparing to take it apart, an enormous pressure strained against it. Panicking I frantically began to rebuild them as fast as I could, an overpowering feeling, it was after me...

But then I slowed. Was it a threat? A force yes, but a threat? Normally when you open yourself up to your surroundings, you'd be lucky to get a few hints of events that had happened. Flashes of emotions, grainy Polaroid's of time past, at best.

I had stood on burial grounds with Nana Tobbot and had felt malevolent spirits and it had been less pressure than I'd just felt against my barrier.

I thought about what was at stake. Raul's freedom. Other girl's lives, perhaps even mine.

Blue, green and yellow blocks – I pushed against the top layer, seeing them fall and disappear. The force against my defenses strengthened, pushing.

One last layer, I pulled it apart, piece by piece. The entity prodded, testing itself against my defenses. Nana Tobbot had spent years teaching me, the only way anything was coming in was if it was powerful beyond my imagination or I unless I was stupid enough to do it my myself.

I guess I was stupid enough.

Sucking in a breath I readied myself to throw up new defenses if I needed too.

Holding the breath I said another silent prayer to the spirits and smashed away my last defenses.

I was open and vulnerable.

Chapter 27

A psychic scream ripped through my head. Falling to my knees I slammed my hands against my ears, trying to rival the screaming in my brain with a helter-skelter vertical dropping yell of my own –a raw throated scream combating the head popping audio explosion I was experiencing as I tried to get control of my own head.

It was too strong.

My eyes flickering at ever increasing speed I felt myself passing out, with a last twitch, a sick feeling in my stomach underscoring what I already knew - I didn't have enough strength to win.

Fading, I pictured my last true line of defense, Nana Tobbot. Falling to the floor I twisted and twitched, kicking out my legs and biting into my tongue as I fought, a seizure tensing up every muscle like a thousand volts.

I felt her coming. The pain had been enough of a sacrifice and I had called her. She had heard me. I tried not to shout out again, grinding my knuckles into my ear as pain lanced deeper into my brain.

I screamed.

But arriving she didn't defend, she calmed. Not me but the entity. The being that was assaulting my spirit and mind, driving me into insanity. But it was doing no good. The anger and anguish from the entity was unbearable, mind crushing. Nana Tobbot's spirit continued to ease and reassure, to near croon at the angry power that was stripping away my mental wellbeing.

She brought out the steel, with a Nana reprimand the onslaught instantly stopped, a petulant twinge brought it back for a moment until it stopped, waiting on the edge of my consciousness.

Nana gave me a small smile, she had done all she could and probably more than she was supposed to. Nana would even bend Heaven's rules if she was of a mind. With a wave she dissipated.

I was left alone with the entity that had almost ripped my brain apart. It waited like a mind bending migraine, its current peaceful disposition perhaps lasting for only moment more.

With a heart that threatened to beat its way out of my chest I struggled to get my body under control. Bringing my legs together I looked up at the vaulted stone ceiling far above as I found my breath.

A sole pigeon crouched on one of the eight arches staring at me like I was its very own channel of MTV. In the last ten minutes I must have put on a real show, no wonder it was standing on one leg, enthralled.

Tensing my stomach muscles I sat, feeling like a sledgehammer had been tapping out the star spangled banner on my forehead and on top of it all – the entity lurked, waiting for me to pull myself together. I could almost feel it tapping its foot with impatience.

Pulling my legs inwards I sat cross legged, my palms up in my lap.

Taking a few deep breaths, I did the equivalent of flipping the closed sign around on the door of my mind and invited the entity inside my head without resistance.

As the being entered I felt fear, disorientation and heart ache, it washed through me and made me hurt but it wasn't the knife in the guts kind of hurt. It was loneliness, regret and chances wasted - when a child loses a parent too soon, when a person is taken before their time, when they've barely lived and have a glorious life ahead. But before they can do anything but see they joy in life, life itself is stolen away.

Then like a light bulb lighting up and going nuclear in my head I realized it all.

She had died on this spot, and worse – she didn't know what had happened to her.

She was afraid, had the memory of pain and didn't know her life was over, all she wanted was to leave Salem Common and go back to her family. She never would. If she was ever to get any peace – I needed to tell her.

When I did, with luck, she wouldn't flip out and tear my mind apart, leave me a babbling mindless idiot. But this wasn't about me – there was a girl my age, who had not grown up lucky enough with her own Nana Tobbot. And she was scared beyond death and powerful to boot.

Chapter 28

I strove for some degree of peace, stamping hard on my own nervousness as the girl visibly appeared in my mind, looking around and taking a tentative step into the mindscape I was struggling to recreate and fast.

Not having the eye of an artist I hadn't managed to pick up every nuance of Salem Common. It's when you really need to recreate what you see –an afterlife might depend on it – when you realize you walk through seeing the world but rarely, truly, seeing it.

The Salem Common mindscape I had hastily built was without detail. Green grass without blades, the trees black balls of cotton candy on sticks– but it was the best I could do without opening my eyes and risk fracturing the mindscape and scaring her off into the void between.

The one image I could create without opening my eyes was my own, appearing by the stone dome – my hand outstretched beckoning. Like a stumbling fawn she walked closer, I looked her over and stifled a gasp as I saw just how similar we were.

Almost sisters, but she was a little shorter and filled out...I had always bordered toward crane like.

The girl looked around, each step forward like she were stepping on fragile ice, no one step a commitment, ready to run in any direction if anything scared her.

"Over here" I said, calling out to her, concentrating on maintaining the world she was so tentatively stepping through.

She flinched and then fully noticed me, waving her forward.

"Where am I? This place is weird." She said, a few more steps bringing her closer.

I didn't know how to answer her. Where are you? Why – you're inside my head of course and oh yeah – you're dead. Fancy a peaceful trip to the afterlife or would you prefer to haunt Salem Common until your spirit finds out who murdered you and can exact some form of excruciating revenge? Your choice – no biggie either way. Okay? Okay.

For the first time in my life I managed to keep my thoughts to myself. Pasting on a smile I spoke to her as reassuringly as I could.

"My name's Sam. What's yours?" I said, in what I hoped was a good non-confrontational first step.

She focused on me properly for the first time, weighing me up, a nearly visible question mark appearing in the creases of her forehead.

"Do I know you?" She said now just a few steps away, looking me up and down. "You look familiar."

My mental self smiled and sat on the steps leading up to the hexagonal platform of the stone gazebo.

"My name is Sam. I don't think we've ever met before, it think I'd remember. What's your name by the way?" I asked.

"Marjorie Blatt. I live just around the corner."

I watched her considered sitting beside me. Marjorie glanced over my shoulder just part of getting settled but as she did her eyes locked on something, sucking in a surprised breath, her face drained of color.

I couldn't help it, even though this was my mindscape and I controlled everything within it, every image, every poorly drawn clump of grass, I still turned, looking over my shoulder. My paranoid mind expecting to see something there but this was my mindscape. It was impossible. There could be no one behind me. Could there? Last glance, last chance – no, there was no one.

But still – she stood there, white faced and my whole recreated world almost blew apart as she spoke,

"You were there. My God, it wasn't a dream. You were there. I thought it was just a nightmare but, but – is it? Tell me. Is this a nightmare? You were there and the wolf. He tried to..."

Her head snapped around, checking every direction.

"There was a wolf." she said, her voice trailing as she scanned the world I'd created in my head.

I felt some relief. She hadn't seen anything, these were the memory remnants from just before she was murdered.

My heart nearly fractured, before I knew it, the imagined me was comforting her. Up close I could see what I hadn't noticed before, she was a little smaller, a little younger than me.

She looked up, eyes wide and watery.

"Where am I? This place is strange? I don't like it..."

A tear fell down the cheek of my real body as I concentrated on keeping it together.

I tried to convince my imagined me to be reassuring, to look at ease, forcing my face to smile, I moved a lock of hair from her face.

"What do you remember?"

She looked around again, but this time as if it would help bring clarity to her memory rather than to reassure herself. She spoke, stumbling over the pieces of memory.

"I was on my way home. Passing by the Common like I always do. Then I felt pulled. I blinked and when my eyes reopened I was already walking across the grass. I wanted to stop. It was scary...and dark but...I couldn't make my legs stop walking." Her face creasing as she struggled to make sense of it.

One moment she had free will and knew exactly where she was going and why, the next, she had moved off her path, and someone else was pulling the strings.

One thing I knew –Werewolves don't take control of their victims. They have a pretty basic approach to werewolfing...change, kill, eat, change back again and if they're lucky run around the forest, marking out their territory, hunt some more and sleep.

Mind control was not part of their bag of wolf tricks.

Giving her shoulder a squeeze I spoke quietly trying to think of as many comforting and peaceful thoughts as I could, not knowing if it would help but trying anyway.

"What happened then? Do you remember anything else?"

She nodded, her top lip quivering.

"I was standing up there..." She pointed up the steps, under the dome. "I was being held, it felt like I had rope around me, I couldn't move, not even a little. I tried." Her voice grew louder. "I tried Sam...I really tried."

My head started to pound with a migraine from hell.

Despite it I smoothed down the back of her hair, leaning her face against my shoulder. I wanted to reassure her more, to tell her everything was going to be okay, but I knew it wouldn't be. I bit my lip struggling to hold in the tears. She had started talking again, explaining,

"...I didn't see who was holding me...I'm not even sure there was anyone – If there had been arms around me I'd have been able to move, even if just a little. But it was like I'd been frozen or locked in place. Then my arms lifted, and I was the one raising them." She looked up at me with wide eyes, "I don't remember any more..."..."

I didn't know the order of events – what had happened, step by step, a big part of me thanked the Gods or Spirits that Marjorie had not experienced the slicing, the cutting of her own murder. But not knowing left her like this. Confused and disorientated.

That was better than the alternative, wasn't it?

"What about the wolf Marjorie?"

She nodded. "It was weird. I didn't know if was a wolf or a man, it seemed confused." She said. "He grabbed me..." then stopped, licking her lips. I squeezed an arm, urging her on. "...he tried to pull me away, to get me out of the center of the hexagon but he couldn't. He wasn't strong enough. Even when I tried to help. I was stuck there, rigid."

"The wolf wasn't holding you?" I said, lifting her chin so I could see her face.

She grinned, "That's silly. How could a wolf hold me?"

But as I didn't grin back she sensed I needed her to tell me as clearly as she could.

Shaking her head, "No. It wasn't the wolf. Something had locked me there before the wolf came. He...I say he but it's an 'it' right? He tried to help not hurt."

It was time to do what I had been dreading. Marjorie. Is that all you remember?"

She concentrated, looking down, creases deepening across her forehead. She began to shake, clasping her arms around chest and pulling tight.

"No. Oh my God. No" her arms flying around me, squeezing. "This can't be happening, it's just some awful nightmare."

Pushing her to arm's length I lowered myself to eye level.

"What Marjorie? What?" my voice urgent.

"They killed me. It killed me."

With surprise spreading across her face she looked around my mindscape as if seeing it for the first time. Understanding it was a fiction, a remembered image and a clumsy rendition at that.

She turned to face me. As she did a darkness passed across her face, manipulating it into a grimace, a red yellow flash of fire flickering almost unnoticeable behind her eyes.

Oh crap!

Chapter 29

"You think you're smart girl?" Marjorie said with a sneer, her voice different, a more gravely resonance, like a deeper voice talking through a throat of rocks.

Her arms encircled my waist again, pulling me closer.

He laughed, a cruel, perverse sound as she pulled me tighter towards herself, grinding her groin into my leg. Leaning forward, faster and stronger than I could push away, she ran her tongue up side my face.

With disgust I pushed her away, her laughter bubbling out, as she chuckled,

"What's the matter Girl? I thought you wanted to get close. To help me." The voice said with a whine, "Well, here I am..." She stuck out her tongue, wiggling it up and down, flicking it left to right lewdly.

"...aren't you going to come and help me now little Sam? Come on Baby – you're cute..."

I took a step back hoping she wouldn't take a step forward. About now would be a great time to be able to recreate those mental barriers I was supposedly so good at creating – no wonder Marjorie had been so strong.

Much stronger than a spirit of only a few hours should be – even if said Spirit had died violently and had a house of horror's worth of fear embedded in their essence. It wasn't just Marjorie inside my head, there was something more. The question was who or what, this side of hell, was it?

Chapter 30

Marjorie laughed at me. It rolled out of her small delicate mouth, the guttural sound totally incongruous with the body and lips it was exuding from.

Head tilted back, mouth opened up to the sky. With a bite of the air, snapping at nothing, Marjorie turned towards me. As she did her skin rippled, moving like cords and muscles were settling, getting comfortable, realigning themselves, like a body experiencing heat haze.

Opening her mouth wide, I almost flinched, one of my eyes half closed and turned away, expecting an alien movie moment, half believing a green black and slimy creature was about to erupt out of her mouth and fly across to attach itself to my face. She yawned then stretched, running a long pink tongue along perfect teeth.

Right. This was my mindscape and it was still my place, I had home turf and I should, by rights, have the edge. I could create, uncreate and break all rational rules inside my head. It was, after all, my imagination.

I jumped up, leaping eight feet in the air, a perfect Bruce Lee moment, my one piece leather suit looking just the part. It felt good. I'd dreamed about this move since I started martial arts when I was still in single year digits. Coming down, my foot extending and aiming straight at her face, I let out a yell, fists clenched.

Trying not to go so far as to buff her nails on her shirt, Marjorie raised a finger and my whole momentum just stopped. No falling, bouncing or slamming against invisible barriers, to make me feel better, I just stopped, frozen in midair feeling pretty ridiculous – like a cheesy lead in a bad Chinese movie.

"Well this is embarrassing" I said through frozen ventriloquist lips, my face locked in a grimace of martial arts intensity as I was held, suspended, above her head.

Marjorie glanced up, acting like she'd noticed me

for the first time.

"Oh, it's you. Sorry, I was thinking about something else." She turned and raised her hand as if gripping an invisible cup. Looking at her outstretched hand, I wondered what was coming.

Marjorie's face scrunched, small lines of concentration and beads of imaginary sweat appearing, her grip around nothing slowly closed. Then I realized what Marjorie was doing, feeling the invisible force constrained me beginning to tighten.

"You know this really is most disagreeable. I let Marjorie have her time. Hoped she would point you in all sorts of interesting directions. But the poor girl and you were smarter than I anticipated. So, here we are. In a bind, forgive the joke."

Marjorie or whatever the heck it was made a show of further closing the space between gripping fingers. I winced, biting down as the pressure crushed and strangled, my spine cracking and twisting while I was locked in midair.

"Why are you doing this? What do you want?" I said straining through the pain.

Marjorie grinned, her smiling predatory, a purple haze played across her constantly undulating face.

"Why? That's an easy one – because I can. After lifetimes contained I am free and I can finally right the wrongs done to my kind."

Her hand twitched and with it, I gasped, more air squeezed from my body.

"What wrong? What could possibly be worth these murders, these deaths?"

Pulling on her chin thoughtfully with her small hand Marjorie stepped close to me running a hand along my thigh, smirking then held her hands out wide and gave a small bow.

"Only a revolution my child and with it, the righting of an injustice my kind has borne since Noah." Her face reformed into Greek tragedy face of sorrow "A few more deaths and we will be ready for the main event. We are getting close – unfortunately for your kind there are more deaths to come...many, many more."

With a gleeful laugh Marjorie's hand closed almost completely, a slight gap between her tensed fingers.

I wanted to struggle, to ask her who her kind were, to get more answers but my air supply was failing, my mind blanking and closing down. Every thought directed at my hands, legs, even fingertips seemed to disappear as soon as they left my brain on their journey to the relevant muscles, failing to arrive.

My chest and lungs felt like I was the cream in a demon Cannoli and if Marjorie's hand kept tightening I'd be squeezed out of each end making one heck of a mess of Salem Common's grass. Hey, I might even get some of my ickyness on Demon Marjorie that would show her, he...it...whatever.

With a grin that would have looked perfect on Tom as he squeezed Jerry, my lungs, heart and intestines met around my compacting spine. I was getting crushed to death and there wasn't anything I could do to stop it. That sucks!

Dammit! This was my mindscape – I created it, drew it, controlled it – this was all wrong, not even the devil himself should have this kind of power in my own mind.

As I struggled to think through the logic, my more critical struggle for oxygen was being lost and without it, my brain was turning off all the switches and getting ready to go leave for all eternity. My synapses were finally getting somewhere. It was a race to figure it out before I passed out –I was losing.

This was my world...my head...[Can't breath]...I control it...[Can't breath]...I can see her hand crushing me...[Can't br...] this is my world...[can't...]

Can't...

Chapter 31

A hand slapped across my face. My brain told me to respond otherwise they'd hit me again. I was too slow. Ouch. Big Déjà vu. Dad?

Blinking away the blackness, the world fell into fragments of one whole image, pieces of light and dark thrown together. Straining to grasp consciousness it felt like a whole cadre of blood vessels had burst in my eyeballs as I tried to Rubik's cube the data presented to my brain.

"Missy. Are you okay? Hello there."

My cheek stung as another slap landed. Whoever came up with the idea of beating someone unconscious into consciousness was an idiot. Fact.

I brought my hand up, my eyes still closed, a clasped a frail wrist joined to a hand travelling towards my face for another slap.

"Enough with the slapping already. How would you like it if I came around your house tonight and slap you silly while you sleep?"

Cracking open a right eye I hoped that was enough of a commitment to waking up to stop the phantom slapper from continuing the onslaught. I left the left closed, eye a rest as my head had a troop of River Dancers playing to a full house inside.

A grizzle bearded man looked down at me, fragments of a green hat perched onto of a head of greasy black hair, his breath smothering me, insisting my left eye join with my right and wake up too.

Whew! Interesting aftershave, Eau De Dumpster.

He leaned in closer, his face inches from my own. I wish he hadn't.

"Missy. You sure you're awake? Want me to slap you again? Happy too if it helps..."

Waving a hand in front of my face, I tried not to wrinkle my nose, whatever this guy smelled like, he'd brought me around. I pushed my smelly white knight back a little, giving myself some space and cough...some fresh air.

"I was watching you. You were just sitting there. You looked weird, like a Popsicle, sort of, frozen. I couldn't see you breathing. Then you just, sort of, fell over. Passed out from what I could tell...didn't mean to hurt you, didn't mean anything by it, I was worried and I've heard that..."

His voice just kept on going as I sat up rubbing the back of my head where Marjorie's mental sledgehammer had obviously connected. Then my fingers probed my cheek where I hit the floor, flakes of Marjorie's blood were stuck to the side of my face. Dusting it off I caught a few words of what the guy was saying.

"Hold it. Say that bit again."

"What? Which bit?"

"About breathing."

He looked at me like I was the mad one, edging a way, in case whatever I was suffering from was contagious. You know you're having a tough day when a hobo thinks you're the crazy one.

"You stopped breathing. I was worried about you suffocating, getting your brain damaged or something. I've heard that it can happen. Haven't ever seen it but..."

That was it. That was what I'd been missing. Marjorie didn't have any more power inside my head than I gave her. She was screwing with me. That's why the cheap Magician theatrics – her hand reaching out, showing me her hand squeezing. My mind did the work. As I thought it, it happened. Passing out, unconscious, no mindscape. No mindscape, no place for Marjorie.

Passing out had saved me. She could have had me opening my veins or worse.

Sitting here, relieved to be alive what did I know?

One. Raul didn't kill Marjorie.

Two. Marjorie had been controlled by a strong, malevolent entity and it was pissed and had an agenda. A revolution, undoing a wrong.

And a little part of my throbbing head gave me a

third point, the creature had resoundingly kicked my butt. It was stronger and if this battle was anything to go by – smarter too.

Slapping down the part of my brain that was being so traitorous, I reminded myself it was just one battle. I was alive, a little battered but I was still in the game.

But I needed help that was for sure.

Noticing that my new friend had stopped talking I looked around, he was kneeling down, looking nervous and concerned, scratching his head, or more accurately, picking something I tried not to visualize from it.

"What?" I asked, not sure if he'd asked me a question.

"So – you're sure you're okay?"

Only time would make me feel better I did my best to put a reassuring smile on my face, hoping it would look better than it felt.

He backed away, my smile must be bordering on manic, I tried to tone it down a little.

"Yeah. Sure. I'm okay." Then I had a thought, reaching inside my leather outfit, pulling out a crinkle cornered leather wallet I'd inherited from my Dad.

"Can I...?" I said, not sure how to say it.

The guy raised a hand, holding up his nose.

"I just helped you out is all. If two people can't help each other out when there's a real problem then we're not real people. Do you know what I mean?" He said, really looking at me, like this was the most important thing he was ever going to say and I was ever going to hear.

I nodded, it did make some sort of basic sense, although I wasn't sure it was as profound as he wanted it to be, but I put on a suitably grave face, pursing my lips and throwing a few creases across my face as my nod repeated itself.

"You're right. And thank you. If there's ever...", my point fading as I realized he lost interest in me, his fingerless gloves diving into the bottom of a wide topped Salem Common trashcan, on the hunt for goodness knows what. Our relationship was obviously at an end, I was worth less than trash to him and given his approach to personal hygiene, I could cope with that. He wouldn't take my money but would spend his time down to his waist in a trash can – and he thought I was the crazy one.

"Crap what time is it?" I said to no one in particular. Rolling my arm to check my watch.

Damn, I was late Mr. Griffin and Louise Conrad. Great. Just great.

I started to run, taking the top step leading to the correctly drawn and defined sunlit Salem Common.

Even though it was a beautiful warm day, part of me was shivering. I'd just had my first battle without Nana Tobbot and I was still holding onto my ass after it had been firmly handed to me by Marjorie or the demon that had been easily toying with me.

I had utterly lost the first battle and for all I knew the next could come at any moment, at the creature's whim.

This time I was lucky, would I be next time?

Taking a step forward I glanced back up towards the trash guy.

A broken yellow crime tape fluttered back at me, the stone platform empty, no helpful grizzled hobo and no trash can. I was alone for as far as my eyes could see. What the…?

Wishing this didn't make my head ache even more than it already did, I resigned myself to the pixies tap dancing in army boots on the top of my skull and focused on getting to my appointment.

Salem was turning into a really fun town.

I'm sure normally you have to drink way too much before you feel this messed up.

Chapter 32

They were both inside when I barged in. The bell above the door going into a frenzied spin as I tripped through the door. Hinges complained as I pushed it closed, probably years since anyone had used this much energy to get at Griffin's books and it was moaning about it.

It was forty-five minutes past. I was officially late. Not politely late but had crossed over the thin line into rudely late territory.

Griffin looked at me from over the top of his half-moon glasses, a round face above a pink and blue spotted bow tie, tied with meticulous fingers.

Meanwhile, Louise stood looking nothing like a Grandmother, the opposite of round, small and friendly, the thought of eating any cookies she'd prepared made me nervous for my ongoing gastric wellbeing. Louise was a women to be reckoned with or better yet, a women to say 'Yes' too before doing exactly as she'd instructed. You could reckon in your own time, not hers.

If Nana Tobbot had an American twin sister with the same steel backbone then she would be Louise's frail younger sister.

She'd asked me to call her Grandma Conrad but to me she looked like a teacher I had back in High School. Tweed skirt, cardigan, pinned up hair, glasses hanging on a chain around her neck. A strong women who had complete control over herself, her immediate vicinity and all she surveyed and despite the glasses, could see further than most.

"Well good afternoon Dear. Nice of you to drop by", Louise said holding out a steaming pink flowered china tea cup.

Taking it I did my best to stop the cup from clinking against the saucer that had snuck underneath it. I'm more of a mug, Dixie cup or a Slurpee kind of person, not given the temperament to handle cups with saucers – call me a Daddy's girl if you like. I held each tightly to the chest of my suit with both hands, if I had a third I'd have used that too.

Blowing off the steam I took a sip. It was the perfect temperature. I may have been forty five minutes late but Louise had known my incoming arrival time to the second.

As if by magic a doorway clicked open in the wood paneling behind the cash register. With a hand gesture Louise offered to let me go ahead. Ducking down a little I glanced sideways as I walked through. The door ran flush with the oak panels that lined the walls of Mr. Griffin's bookshop, just about invisible when closed.

Navigating the horrendously steep staircase leading up, an empty space and sunlight was visible above.

As my head cleared the floor I kept on stepping through the opening, I was in one of the most perfectly beautiful rooms I've ever seen. Sunlight streamed through high windows bathing well varnished wooden floors and the occasional intricate rug, the designs minute and challenging to the eye.

Where the windows ended the bookcases began, every wall filled with upright and horizontally stacked books, their ends creating a collage of muted colors. Crimson ends blending with browns, tans with blacks and the occasional red thrown in for visual spice.

Stepping up through the space in the floor, a beeswax smell of the wood polish bound together with a hint of pipe tobacco and lavender, soothing me despite still balancing the tea cup on its saucer.

Four mismatched arm chairs but two stood out. One leather, aged and comfortable, the other, a clear cut, firm edged traditional flower print.

Despite the books and the comfort, my eyes were drawn to the room's center, a circular dark wood table sat etched with numerous shapes and alphabets, candles evenly spaced and lit. Snakes of smoke bursting occasionally as the air in the room shifted. Between the candles was a map. Edging closer, holding the cup and saucer tighter, I leant forward. Taking an absentminded sip of the still hot tea.

It was a map of Salem. A black kohl pencil had marked an 'X' on Salem's Common. Scanning I stopped at another 'X'. Salem Acres. Leaning closer still I found three more but smaller. Two on places I just didn't know, the last I did.

The Bookshop of Horror.

Louise was behind me as I stood up straight. Either I was getting exceptionally bad at the whole sensing part of being a witch or I was seriously outclassed. I knew which it was and thankfully I was still on her good side. I hadn't even heard her come up the stairs.

Mr. Griffin's head was just poking up through the hole in the floor. It was a little disconcerting to see him materializing like that from the floor.

"Ah...Yes. The map. Well, I guess it saves all the unpleasant preamble." Louise said "and from wasting yet more time. Time is a commodity in short supply." She flicked a finger towards a chair, "please sit down. Although we don't have much time, if we have to break eggs better we make the best omelet we can."

I decided to just throw it all out there and see what happened. Sliding the tea cup onto the middle table they both watched me, waiting.

"It wasn't a werewolf. There's something else involved and I'm pretty sure it's not a werewolf." I said.

Louise smiled, glancing at Griffin who looked thoughtful, taking a pipe off a side table and giving it a chew without lighting it.

"I told you she was smart Griffin. Didn't I tell you?"

"Yes Louise. You did say she was smart", teeth clicking on the stock of the pipe. "But I wonder if you're both too smart for your own good. Somewhere the werewolves are up to their snouts in this one."

Shaking my head I thought of Raul. Of what Marjorie had said before she had gone demonic on me – that Raul had tried to help her, to pull her away. I had to hope that part was the real Marjorie and not just lies told by the entity that had used me as a squeeze toy.

Swinging my legs up on the arms of the chair I picked at nail,

"Now I don't know much about werewolves. In fact, I know nothing more than they're people who change into wolves and back again. But is mind control part of their shtick?" I asked, glancing between them both.

Louise raised an eyebrow, "Their...shtick?" her eyes twinkled a little, "No. Not that I know...Griffin?"

He shook his head, "No, that's not part of their...um ...shtick. It's a lot more basic than that as you can imagine."

"Well right then. Marjorie told me that..."

Taking her feet off the foot rest, Louise leaned forward, her hands placed precisely onto each of the chair's fat leather arms.

"Marjorie?" She glanced at Griffin before looking back. "Marjorie told you what dear?"

I sucked in a breath and held it counting to ten in my head. Looking between Griffin and Louise, I made it to six.

"What?" I said to Griffin. He shrugged.

"What? What?" I turned to Louise.

Louise coughed a little, putting her already perfect hair back into place.

"Well a friend at the Police Station told us that Marjorie was found early this morning. I'm not sure if she's a friend of yours Dear but I have some news. I'm afraid it's not good news."

Her mouth turned down as she leant across to put a long fingered hand on my arm. The mind boggled. When I'd last seen her she was dead and it looked very much like her spirit had been taken over by a mind-blowingly powerful demon. How much worse could it be for poor old Marj?

"Bad news? There's worse?" I asked staring into her face intently. She tried to digest my sentence, confused. She pushed on forward as she was want to do when in doubt.

"Yes Dear. I'm afraid so. Marjorie is...well, she's dead Dear..." She said giving my arm a little squeeze.

I couldn't help it, after the last forty hours of pure stress, this misunderstanding was the closest to humor I'd come in days.

What started as a crack in my face became a grin, that grin was chased away by a lopsided smile, which was slapped aside by a lung busting laugh. Throwing my head back I let it out, an African Hyena would have been proud. After a good thirty seconds or so I sucked it back in, wiping away tears and still hiccupping.

Biting down firmly on the end of his pipe Griffin's eyebrows were up into his hairline. He muttered under his breath as I stilled my laughter.

"Well I never" he said with a humph and caught Louise's eye.

Louise gave me a little smile in return for my guffaws, shrugging back at Griffin before standing.

"She already knew. When you said you spoke with Marjorie. You mean after she was killed. Isn't that what you meant Sam?" She didn't wait for me to answer speaking across the room to Griffin.

My laughter started again, it was verging on hysteria only enhanced as Griffin continued to chew on his pipe, not registering that it was outside of his mouth and being held in a slack hand by his side.

I was tired, frightened and had been on a permanent House of Horror joy ride for the last forty eight hours. I needed to snap out of it.

Louise saw as much in the depths of my eyes, stepping forward, she snapped her fingers in front of my face. My laughter stopped like a switch thrown.

"Now that's quite enough of that Dear don't you think?"

I couldn't have agreed more, any longer and I'd have made my own personal contribution to the room's look and feel, it would have been colorful but not pleasant.

I took a deep breath.

"You can't blame us you know?" she said. "We had understood you were a witch. A powerful one but we had no idea. No idea at all...did we Mr. Griffin?"

I raised my hand to stop them there, knowing if I didn't stop it as soon as I started to feel lost, I'd never find my way back to any place that made sense.

"Hold it a sec..." I stood, walking over to the window and looking out over the street below, holding onto the vision of the trees spaced along the sidewalk and cars passing by reassuring me the world still had some constants.

Turning back around, Griffin and Louise were both waiting for me, looking to each other.

"You say you knew I was a witch?" I asked, both Louise and Griffin nodded but kept quiet.

"How?"

"You have power dear. As soon as you came to town you appeared like a small sun. Sort of disturbing the flow for a day or two until it shifted a few things around..."

Chewing my lip I tried to make sense of all she had just said and satisfied myself with understanding about half. I had power – check. I knew I came to Salem because of this power – check (sort of). The rest – I'd ask her to explain when we had more time.

"You said you thought I was a witch but I couldn't blame you for getting that wrong. Either I am or I'm not. Discuss."

"What do you know about Witches Dear?"

Lifting up my hand I started to count off my fingers.

"Spells, black cats, pointy hats, broom sticks..."

She looked at me under hunched eyebrows disapprovingly. "Yes very funny Dear. What do you really know about Witches?" barely trying to keep the frustration from her voice and failing horribly at that too.

Counting off from my first pinky again.

"In tune with nature, believe in the Golden Rule, the law of threefold return and the Rede - if it harms none, do what you will. Then we probably get into the cloudy area of spells, incantations and dancing around in the middle of the night in your nightdress or less. How's that?"

A frown played around on Louise's face, shaking her head as tutted under her breath.

"I can't believe Tobbot taught you that...that...claptrap. Tobbot went to one of the better places of learning, she wouldn't pass on such rubbish to you, even in jest. 'If it harms none, do what you will' is not the rede of the witch. It's the rede of Wiccans. They are not necessarily the same Girl."

Ooops, she has resorted to calling me 'girl' – that can't be good. I leant against the window sill, sitting on my hands and trying to show I was all ears, Ms. Attentive.

She'd opened a wooden box sitting beside her, her fingers hidden inside and resting.

"Being a witch is an honorable profession Ms. Ray. It comes closest to being the village medicine women before the Science Religion came along and usurped our position. With Wicca's the common thread between them is there is no common thread. No central set of beliefs except that last babble you spouted. The Rede – if it harms no one blah blah blah. Frankly I'd rather you kept answering my question spouting about black cats and pointy hats."

Clearing his throat Griffin got our attention, pulling the pipe out of his mouth with a slight pop.

"We don't have time for this Louise. We can go through the differences between Wiccan's and Witches when life is a shade slower. Let's get to the point shall we."

With her mouth half open I could see her mentally running through a harsh response – people didn't tend to get away with hurrying her. But after a slight thoughtful hesitation she nodded.

With a mild gulp I walked back and sat down on the foot stool by her feet. If she could be closed down in mid-pontification about the trials and tribulation of witches then not only was this deathly serious (which I already knew) but we must also be under some intense time pressure too.

"You're right. I apologize to both of you." She gave Griffin a small smile before turning back to address me. "The point I was going to make Dear was you are a witch – Fact. But also a fact – Witches don't tend to converse with the dead dear. That falls into a different set of abilities and power. You have the hints of real power but it's not constraining itself to the usual areas, let's just say it's manifesting itself in a few...unorthodox ways."

Shuffling forward on the foot stool I glance between Griffin and Louise.

"The usual areas?" I asked, almost to hear the answer.

"Yes Dear. It's not easy to explain but let me see if I can simplify it."

"That would be nice..." I said with worried sarcasm, I hate it when my mouth operates before my brain had time to catch up.

She hesitated, a glimmer of either humor or anger in the back of her eye.

"Quite Dear. Put simply – witches are about life, nature, emotions, spells, natural medicines, using the white arts and so on. Necromancy is about the summoning of spirits, demons, death, black arts, the base emotions - anger, fear, lust."

Louise pulled her hand out of the box it had been resting in throwing an object towards me.

Catching it in midair, I opened my hand. Sitting on my palm was a coin.

"It's for you. A gift...of sorts." She said.

On one side of the coin made from gold or bronze was a tree, its limbs intertwined and encircling the solid trunk, heavy round fruit dotted throughout. It spoke to me of the abundance of life and growth, of hot summer days and the smell of cut grass.

Flipping the coin it looked like it had been carved from black stone or iron. A similar tree but this one bare and skeletal, bare of fruit, a skull grinning, from the emaciated trunk, a snake entwined and strangling from the ground to the branch limbs. A sickly oily feeling rolled around my stomach just looking at it, made me want to scratch a termite itch.

"What the hell is this?" I asked them. Pulling out his pipe Griffin opened his mouth, Louise filled it with her own voice.

"It's the Coin of Life Dear."

"But the other side is ghastly..."

"...it's also the coin of death dear. They are intertwined but separate. Sides of the same coin..."

"Ah...I get it. Witches are one side of the coin..."

"Necromancers the other side. Yes Dear. But we have a teensy complication...."

"A...teensy....complication?" I said swallowing, not believing I'd just said that word but ignoring it as I suspected I knew what was coming next and it wasn't good.

"Yes dear...you seem to be both. That's..."

"Different." Griffin said, jumping into the conversation staring resolutely at Louise.

Noticing she let out a breath then smiled. "Yes, Mr. Griffin is right. You are...different. Tobbot said as much..."

Taking my eyes off the coin I quickly looked at Louise, wondering when her relationship with my mentor, Louise's green eyes firm, small laughter lines tweaking her lips, suggesting she could smile when lives didn't hang quite so in the balance. I knew how she felt.

"Yes Dear, I know Nana Tobbot. Let's just say we were pen pals, we can talk about this when we have more time. Sorry but we have to go." She said standing, and began pulling what looked like Sunday Garage sale bric-a-brac into a straw bag.

"Go?"

"Yes go. The two murders you experienced. If we are correct, they are just the beginning and you my Dear, are on the list."

"There's a list?"

"Well I'm not sure if there's an actual list but there certainly a logic behind what's happening. An intelligence behind what seemed, initially, like disparate occurrences. When you arrived in Salem the speed of activity increased, like the agenda had been brought forward. You're in real danger."

Tell me something new I thought as I blew my fringe in exasperation.

Chapter 33

Making sure the life side was closest to my skin I dropped the coin of life and death inside my breast pocket.

Chewing my lip I asked no one in particular.

"Where are we going?"

Louise stopped her packing. "Somewhere safe. We don't want them to get you too."

"Them?"

She got busy again, more bits of stuff being pulled into the never full bag, ignoring my question.

I took a hold of her forearm.

"Them?" I said, louder this time.

She stopped instantly, her eyes in the bottom of the bag before she met mine a moment later.

"The Dark Brotherhood of Sammael"

My hand dropped from her arm, she tried to smile with some reassurance, but she did a poor job of it taking a shaky breath.

"They have a name? Why didn't anyone tell me they had a name? If they have a name then they're real. Who the hell are they? Dungeons and Dragon fanatics? Some Comic Con Gang? Never heard of them. Why have I never heard of them and what do they have to do with me?"

"With you Dear? Nothing in particular, aside from needing your blood for some obscure rite to fully bring their master back into the world. And they would be overjoyed to kill him," she nodded toward Griffin, his back to us as he hummed a tune to himself, "...and me to get to you."

"But why me?" I said, teenager petulance adding a whine even I could hear as I spoke.

"Let's not whine. Let's just get out while we still have time..."

I stamped my foot. "No. I'm not going anywhere." kicking the foot stool over then, seeing Louise's lips purse as she looked from me to the footstool I jumped forward and stood it back upright.

She waited for me to finish then kicked it over.

"I recommend next time you want to make a point with my furniture – you don't stand it back up afterwards. It reduces the dramatic impact don't you think?

I looked at her, trying not to smile. This women was good.

For the first time since coming upstairs Louise smiled, then, praise everything holy, she laughed. Dropping the bag on the floor, taking me by the shoulder with one elegant hand.

"So you don't want to run and hide?" She said, her eyes playful.

Griffin turned and gave me a wink, they had both been waiting for me to make up my mind. Bastards.

I shook my head. "No".

"You're sure?"

I nodded.

"Certain – no matter what?" Louise's green eyes holding onto me as a jumping bean flip flopped in my stomach.

I nodded again, not sure exactly what I was agreeing too.

"No. I need to hear you say it. Otherwise I'll drag your ass out of this room, down those stair and into the car myself. And don't think I couldn't do it..." She said, her voice iron as she cracked her knuckles.

This bird was unbelievable.

My voice coughed out of my chest, much louder and more forceful than even I expected.

"I'm not going anywhere damn it. And I sure as shit am not running away – especially from anyone who call themselves the Brotherhood of Sammael. I'm mean – what a name. They sound like a bad seventies rock group or something."

Louise looked me up and down, past the leather suit, the short dyed hair, the nose stud, all of it for a brief moment I felt like she truly saw me and she wasn't completely unimpressed. Then she frowned.

"First – there is no need to use expletives dear. It doesn't make the point more strongly and it certainly isn't ladylike. Second, the brotherhood of Sammael are Necromancers. Perhaps the most powerful the world has seen in the last two centuries. And even if we're not going to run and hide – we should still get out of here. Griffin...the Keeper..."

He grabbed a brown felt hat dropping it onto his round head. "Yes Louise."

"Go get Bessy. We'll be right down."

"Yes Louise." He said, already walking down the stairs to the shop below, his pipe bouncing as he lowered himself into the floor.

"Where are we going?" I asked.

"To see a man about a book"

"What kind of book?"

"The Book of Demons. Now take this." She said handing me a brown paper bag.

I hefted the bag, feeling its weight and listening to the items moving inside.

"What's in here? Items for summoning...Incense, Holy water. That sort of thing?"

"Not exactly dear."

Taking a peek inside I lifted my head out in disgust.

"Cookies?"

She grabbed a long jacket of a standing coat rack and started to disappear down the stairs. Chasing behind her she called up the stairwell.

"Just in case we get peckish later."

"Peckish – what kind of word is that?" I said under my breath as I started to walk down.

Her voice from the shop below, "It means hungry dear."

Red faced I came to the bottom. Griffin and Louise stood ready, coats on, looking like a couple of Librarians let out from the archives for good behavior. These two were my protectors? Oh Brother was I in big trouble.

"Will...you...stop...calling...me...Dear." I said.

Louise opened her mouth to speak but before she did I raised my hand to stop her.

"You're going to say "Yes dear" aren't you?" from between mock clenched teeth.

Louise grinned shaking her head.

"No Dear, I was going to say 'Pass the Cookies'."

I shoved the brown paper bag towards her and glad to be taking the first step, I pulled open the bookshop door ready to walk out.

"So, off to see a man about a book of Demons eh?"

Without waiting or responding, Griffin rattled his car keys and walked straight past saying "Time to see Bessy", open mouth Louise breezed past with a "Yes Dear" and a tap under my chin to stop me catching flies.

I hopped and skipped to catch up.

Chapter 34

Griffin unlocked and opened a green garage door, a dust cloud belching out as the air found its way in. Inside, a thick crinkly sheet was thrown across an object of curves and dust.

"My God, this is a health hazard" walking around and trying to peek under Bessy's skirt. Small round wheels and edges of little silver tarnished hubcaps were just visible underneath.

Grabbing hold of the sheet Griffin bit down on his pipe's stalk.

"Stand back Ms. Ray. I am about to unveil a marvel of modern engineering..."

With a whoosh he pulled the sheet off like a Magician. A dust storm exploded over us, leaving Griffin with instant white hair and eyebrows, Louise a hand shape across her mouth and me, coughing and spitting onto the concrete floor.

I blinked through the sparkling cloud of particles. A round little grass green sat, wood trimming its edges. Running my hand over Bessy's smooth bonnet I trailed my finger over a chrome emblem, an inverted Nike swoosh with a letter 'M' in the center. I didn't have a clue what kind of strange car this was but it was kind of cute.

"Modern engineering? Modern to who? The settlers of Salem?" I said, only half joking but giving her a little stroke in case I hurt her feelings.

Griffin made a humphing noise under his breath, got in and leant across to open the passenger door. Louise got in and closed the door behind her.

Waiting for one of them to let me in, I arched an eyebrow as Griffin wound down his window.

"Sorry – this is a two-seater. You'll need to jump in the back. It's a nice flat surface, great for storage and you can take a nap if you get tired..." nodding over his shoulder to Bessy's rear.

Grumbling to myself I walked around, and pulling

the two rear doors open, slid inside. Sitting cross legged, I faced out of the two back doors, giving them the benefit of a few whispered navy curse words as I shuffled around, trying to get comfortable.

With a toot toot from a horn that would have been more fitting from a peddle bicycle with a basket, we were off. Slowly.

Purple and black smoke belched out the exhaust creating a haze almost impossible to see through the back window. With a cough I settled back on one elbow, hoping I wouldn't be wiped out by Carbon Monoxide poisoning when there were so many more interesting and exotic methods of killing me today.

Complaining of the inhuman treatment it took me only twenty minutes to realize I had the whole back to myself and a tartan picnic blanket was folded in the corner. Two minutes after the revelation, I was lying down, tucked up and asleep.

Maybe an hour at most of bone shaking semi-sleep later I sat up, remembering where I was just in time not to crack my head on the low roof of the little English car.

The fact that we'd been travelling for a while was obvious when I awoke by the differences outside of the window. We had definitely moved from town to Suburbia to countryside. Townhouses and shops were replaced by fields, a single lane road, hedges, clusters of trees and to a Navy Base brat, the noisy silence of the countryside.

It had also moved from daylight to early evening, the bright day's sunlight smothered by lengthening shadows which would grow and multiple until the day suffocated. We drove away from our homes and towards the night.

"Where are we?" running my hand through my messed hair, stifling a yawn.

Louise stayed eyes front, her hands crossed perfectly on her lap like she was in church rather than in a fight against demons and necromancers.

"Does it matter dear?" She said, a firmness toying

with the edges of her lips.

"Just passing the time while we get to where it is we're going. And I have a right to know don't I?"

"Of course you do."

I waited for her to speak two minutes of silence later realized I'd be waiting for a temperature drop in Hades if I tried to get what I wanted from Louise by acting like a petulant child.

Trying to keep a sulky tone out of my voice I asked her again,

"Louise, would you mind telling me where we're going pretty please?"

"Not at all dear. I think I already told you that we're going to see a man about a book. Well that's exactly where we're going. The exact location is less important than the 'why?' of it."

I thought about that then asked "So why are we going?"

The day was ending and we were being chased by lengthening shadows as we drove as quickly as we could towards the retreating sun.

Louise looked in all directions glancing around until satisfied. She twisted towards me in her seat.

"Have you heard of a man called John Dee?" She asked, watching me closely like she was expecting some light bulb glow of recognition to pass across my face. I was almost sorry I was going to disappoint.

I shook my head. "No, never heard of him. Is that who we're going to meet?"

"Let's hope not dear. Mr. Dee has been dead for almost four hundred years."

I shrugged. "Nothing would surprise me anymore."

Somehow I'd hit on the right thing to say as Louise rewarded me with a grin.

"Maybe you'll get through this in one piece after all dear."

"I sort of hoped so. Tell me about Mr. Dee" I asked as I crossed my legs.

"He was an Advisor to Elizabeth I."

I looked at Griffin's back and could see that despite driving he was listening, and had become completely still.

"As in the English Elizabeth I – Sir Walter Raleigh, the coat over the puddle...that Elizabeth I?"

She smiled, pleased.

"The same. John Dee was a brilliant man – scientist, astronomer, advisor and Occultist."

"Occultist?" I looked at her sharply "You mean the Queen of England's scientific advisor was a Black Magician?" I said, disbelief creeping into my voice.

"Yes dear, he even divined the day of Queen Elizabeth's Coronation to have the most favorable spirits watching over her and her reign. He was very influential."

My chin dropped at the thought of the Queen of England being guided by a Black Magician.

Louise turned towards the front of the car and gave Griffin a momentary look.

"Almost there" he said.

She turned back and continued speaking.

"You have to remember that the sciences weren't as clear cut and nicely packaged in those days. They were all bundled together, one big subject – later some became 'legitimate', others less so. "

"So he studied the planets? Turning lead into gold? What?"

"Not exactly. He summoned and spoke with angels and demons predominantly."

"Wow. Summoning demons. I can see it's so close to chemistry and the other sciences, it's amazing it isn't part of a University course somewhere – seems perfectly legitimate."

Griffin gave me a pleased grin in the mirror before focusing back on the road.

"But I still don't get where John Dee comes into this?"

"There's no need for sarcasm dear." She said with a look of reproach. "He had a book. A Grimoire, that's what we call a book of spells or incantations. He used it to summon demons."

"But if he's an advisor to Elizabeth I, I assume he's English and died there. So the book is in England or am I wrong?"

We turned off the single track onto an even more primitive road, my head banging against the roof of the car as we bounced our way along the lane, hitting every dip and worn cleft in the muddy road.

"Yes dear, you're wrong. Mr. Griffin and I believe the Keeper has Dee's spell book."

"The Keeper, who's he?"

"It's just like it sounds dear. He keeps items safe...and he lives", her finger prodded out of the window, "...here". Betsy stopped, her springs creaking as she rocked in place, coming to the conclusion we had stopped travelling and should stop moving, eventually.

"What kind of car is this anyway?" I asked one hand leaning against a large elm tree as I got out of Bessy.

Griffin ran his hand around the large black nobly steering wheel an infatuated doe eyed expression on his face. Sighing he pulled out the longest key I've ever seen, lowered the sun visor and closed it on top of the keys, tight against the roof.

Standing outside he gave it a small pat as if it were an old friend.

"It's a 1960 Moggie from England. Isn't she a beauty?" He said, pride in his voice.

"Sure she is, you're going to leave your keys in the car like that?"

He swept his hand around, we were standing in a clearing surrounded by forest, most of humanity miles in any direction. I got his point.

Before I could think of a smart answer I looked up the driveway towards the house we stood below all words dropping from my mind.

The house itself wasn't particularly ominous, architect had obviously watched psycho and decided to create a giant sized version of the house in stone. It was a dark and brooding face, the windows stared at us while a drawbridge and door were eager to swallow us whole. Like I said, not ominous at all.

We clomped across the drawbridge and peering down, I was only half surprised large crocodiles with red glowing eyes weren't looking hungrily back licking their lips.

Taking hold of the Satan faced metal door knocker Griffin let it fall with its own weight. That was enough. We heard and felt the sound reverberate as echoes through the inside of the house.

We waited the dank and putrid moat water stank while gnats buzzed trying to make a run our bare necks.

A feeling like I was being watched crawled up around my neck and sat by my ear whispering, insisting I rubberneck looks over my shoulder every few seconds try to see whatever was giving me the heebie jeebies.

I had a really bad feeling and I just couldn't shake it.

Chapter 35

"Whoever you are come out. I know you're watching us..."

The bushes, trees and birds of the countryside opted for silence, waiting for the watcher to make up its mind.

Then an apple came from the closest clump of shrubs straight and true, hitting me painfully in the chest before I had a chance to move aside. Juice splattered on the leather surface, small fragments of mashed apple remained as the majority fell to the floor.

"Ouch – right, that's it."

I dove into the undergrowth. As I got my head below the leaves and branches I caught sight of what looked like child's legs running between the brambles. They disappeared before I could right myself, crouching down, scuff and skid marks in the dust showed me the way my fruit attacker had fled. Bending down below the canopy of leaves and thorns, I did my best to follow.

Pushing aside strips of wild raspberry, thorns that dangled down across my path made scratches across my palms. I couldn't see anyone and had lost all sense of direction. Dammit. Peering down at the floor I saw more tracks or...maybe I didn't, in this light it was getting impossible to tell.

Standing straight up I brought my head through the leaves, a shoulder above the wild berry bushes. No more than ten feet away stood Griffin smoking his pipe, Louise stood calmly, hands together waiting and a man who would pass for a fantasy novel dwarf, down to the green tights and point felt shoes – very Tolkien but thankfully without the armor, axes and broadswords. He stood picking his teeth beside Griffin and Louise who hadn't moved since I'd jumped in to chase the small legs – the legs which plainly belonged to him.

Boy was I making a good impression.

Disregarding the thorns I pushed my way through

the brambles until I stood in front of them, downhearted and feeling ridiculous.

Holding out a bloody scratched hand I said,

"You must be the Keeper I'm Sam. Sam Ray."

He grinned, took taking my hand and gave it a firm shake. As our hands locked I felt a jolt, not painful, more like a deep part of me reacting in sharp recognition.

I wasn't sure but he seemed to feel it too, not letting go he raised an eyebrow, turned his head to the side, and looking at me anew.

"You are welcome Ms. Ray." He said, his voice deep and warm. "Shall we go inside?"

Louise, Griffin and I walked a step or two behind the Keeper who, despite his stature, never seemed to be rushing or making an effort to stay ahead of us. I ran my fingers along the large stone blocks that framed the overshadowing wooden door.

Without stopping the Keeper kept walking, the door opened into a gray stone hallway of its own accord, tapestries of halo bright Saints making hand-clasped prayers to the heavens, adorned the walls. Two iron multi-headed standing candlesticks stood, a suspended matching chandelier, white tallow candles lit the room, darkness and light warring across the walls with each minute flicker.

Louise stood just inside the doorway and sniffed, a slight whistle came from beneath Griffin's red gold moustache as he appreciated the room. The Keeper seemed pleased with our awe but then he focused on Louise as she gave a not so quiet 'tut'.

He moved from foot to foot as he seemed to read her mind.

"Too much?" He said frowning as he looked around the room and its trappings as if seeing it for the first time.

She shrugged as if it were all nothing to her, hardly even worth mentioning.

"It's too much isn't it?" said he said his shoulder's slumping.

Casting her hands to the side with a 'whatever you think best' look across her face.

The Keeper nodded. "I thought it was too much. I always seem to vie on towards Gothic but I've been going through a bit of a Hitchcock phase –I would have opting more towards Country Cottage but it takes so long to concentrate on all that straw..."

Raising his hands he clicked his fingers.

The stone hallway, tapestries, candles and in fact the whole house ceased to exist with a pop my ears felt.

Standing slack mouthed and wanted dearly to rub both of my eyes with my knuckles and give my brain time to catch up with the tricks being played on it. If that building had been an illusion it was so intricate, so compelling it defied what was possible. My hand stroked the column around the door – the stone blocks had been rough and real on my fingertips. I checked them out, there was still dust and grime on them. It was no illusion. But they also just disappeared and there were no camera crews, white tigers or television magicians smiling with immaculate teeth.

So what the hell?

Louise brought her hand up to her mouth, stifling a yawn.

She looked bored as she pulled her cardigan close around her, straightening her clothes and giving the barest look at the place where the house was no more.

Griffin winked before tapping the edge of his pipe on his shoe's sole, knocking out the embers long since dead.

Just in case I was starting to become less disoriented, which obviously wouldn't do at all, my ears tingled and with another pop we stood outside a different door. Either we were teleporting or this was a whole different door, and house. Glass frosted and wood paneled, a brass '73' above its knocker.

Looking up and around it, , we now stood outside a yellow bricked house, vines stretching up and around white windows, a gray slated roof, a bicycle padlocked with heavy silver chain against the wall, a basket trash left inside it.

Stretching out my fingers, this time it was sandstone flaking against my fingers, leaving behind sand residue on the swirls of my fingertips. One of the gutters around the roof had a long time leak, the water drops having eroded a hand sized scoop in the flagstone, green algae coalescing. This had stood here for three hundred years or I was going mad.

Louise undid one of the buttons on her cardigan and nodded with raised eyebrows. The Keeper beamed as if he'd been patted on the head and told 'good boy'.

"Let's go inside and get comfortable" Louise said and without waiting pushed the door open, striding into a hall of sunlight, wood wormed chairs and pot pouri – personally I preferred the Gothic building but thought it best to keep that to myself.

Strolling to the sitting room she found a perfectly situated armchair and sat down, we filed through after her.

When we were all settled the Keeper picked up a glass of lemonade which had appeared out of nowhere, taking a long satisfying gulp. Feeling disconcerted I just about jumped to the ceiling with nails holding me there like a petrified cat as I realized a glass sat beside my elbow. It had absolutely not been there before and no one had brought it, quietly or otherwise. This Keeper guy was starting to freak me out.

Trying to get a non-shaking grip I picked it up, splashing a little glass clinking against my teeth. Louise was my antithesis, she sat perfectly relaxed, legs crossed, tweed skirt and cardigan arranged just so. Not one hair out of place.

"You've come about the book." The Keeper said without any preamble. "How much does she know?" he asked Louise as if Griffin and I had out ears amputated at birth.

Louise spoke, reinforcing my disconnectedness, by giving no indication we were listening, never once looking away from the Keeper.

"We started to go into what we surmised as we travelled here."

The Keeper snorted, "You can surmise all you like. I've been keeping it safe all these years and I know. Its time has come again."

Griffin spoke, his voice quiet and calm.

"We believe the Grimoire belonged to John Dee, Occultist to Elizabeth I. Some of my initial research seems to prove it. But..."

The Keeper tried not to smirk, "...But you don't know what it does or how it came to the Order. Perhaps I can show you..."

Our surroundings changed. Well, that's not entirely accurate – there was no process of change. We were sitting in armchairs drinking homemade lemonade, then we weren't. We were sitting watching life unfold.

Piled bedclothes in a four-poster bed with thick, moth chewed burgundy velvet hanging from spiraling walnut beams between each post. A bowlful of grapes, a few lonely peaches rendered in a gilt edged oil painting at the foot of the bed. Inside it, thin arms lay almost unnoticed across a large leather bound book and floating above it, a white whiskered face in need of moisture below a soft cotton white and blue stripped night cap.

Kneeling beside was a man I'd seen too often in history books.

Without thinking I spoke,

"That's Sir Walter Raleigh, what's he doing here? Is this a movie set?"

With a shush Louise shook her head and tried to stand in front of me – the whispered conversation between the frail man and Sir Walter faltered. They looked about the room, looking disconcerted. I held my breath. A moment later they turned back to one another, slight shrugs.

I let out my breath slowly and quietly, we were standing right there but thankfully for their sanity and mine, we could not be seen, best we keep it that way.

The Old man lifted his arm from off the book, a signal that they had an agreement. Sir Walter darted forward and grasping. Clasped it to his chest it's cover flashed silver. Raleigh stood, a hand loosening from Dee's Grimoire, his fingers scratching the back of his neck involuntarily. His legs moved fast, leaving the room, he never once looked back. The elderly man rested back on his pillow, settling his arms on top of his bedclothes, letting out a long breath, some relief in his relaxed slouch.

The scene glimmered and rearranged.

A much older looking Sir Walter, his shrunken and gaunt hands offering a package wrapped in a rough sacking cloth,

"A gift for you to speed me on my journey. I would gift it before I die, am dressed and put to rest. I hope it gives you as much as it has given me. May God have mercy on your soul."

He knelt then just as when we'd seen him in the bedroom moments but decades before. This time he knelt resting his chin over a stained and grooved wooden block, his neck rested in the crease of it, he looked up. A black hooded executioner, wide eyes darting behind the holes in semi-darkness,

"At this hour, my ague comes upon me. I would not have my enemies think I quaked from fear." Seeing the axe that would behead him, he said "This is a sharp Medicine, but it is a Physician for all diseases and miseries". Giving a released breath of relief akin to the elderly man in the bed who had bequeathed the book to him. Signaling with his eyes he said his last words - "Strike, man, strike!"

With no pause, the axe struck, a slight resistance as the rounded heavy blade met Sir Walter's spine. Then his head fell, rattling around the straw lined basket. After sixty six years of being together, the head did not immediately realize it had left its body behind. Licking his lips, he tried to remove a stray piece of straw before a hot spurt of blood coming from the now headless body splashing it. Its disconnectedness no longer in doubt, Sir Walter's eyes rolled up into his head.

The executioner did his best to step back but not

quickly enough. Sir Walter Raleigh's blood splashed across his black mask – some splashes even passing through the eye holes. Gasping and seemingly struggling for breath the executioner did the unthinkable, he raised his hood showing a young, peaked face, streaks of bloody tears running from his eyes.

His face was familiar –but that was impossible, how could I know the executioner of Walter Raleigh?

He wiped the blood away with his sleeve but traces of blood remained as if they refused to be wiped clean.

Picking up the wrapped package he'd just been given by the murdered Sir Walter, he turned, staggering, shoving his way through the resistant crowd. Just as he disappeared amongst the faces in the crowd he looked back and I knew that face, I'd seen it often since I'd moved to Salem.

Roger Conant, Salem's founder, had Dee's Grimoire.

Chapter 36

The Keeper caught my eye and with a chuckle we were back in the sandstone house, Louise and Griffin frowning, my mind threatening to shut down through sensory overload.

Louise shook her head, the disagreement etched in every line across her face.

"Show us the past if you will but history tell us that John Dee's library was ransacked before his death while he was in Europe travelling. There's no proof Conant had Dee's Grimoire."

Scratching his black stubble beard he smirked. "Well yes and no. I have the Grimoire and it was Dee's. So that point is mute. Our Order debated if Dee's Grimoire would unlock the meaning of the Voynich Manuscript or was just a standalone Grimoire in its own right?"

I'd had enough of sitting on the sidelines while the adults had their cryptic conversations – the day's when I only speak when I'm spoken to have long since passed – if they even ever truly existed.

"OK folks – I have pieces but not the whole picture wh..."

"Welcome to our world young lady..." the Keeper interrupted.

Raising his hand Griffin fixed the Keeper with a stare and miracles amongst miracles – the Keeper closed his mouth, mimicking turning a key in front of his mouth before throwing it away.

"Go ahead my Dear." Mr. Griffin said.

"Thanks. So, was that Roger Conant? Was that a spell book? And what the hell is the Voynich manuscript and what does it have to do with any of this craziness?"

There was complete silence. Louise shuffled with some discomfort in her chair, Griffin reached inside his jacket pocket and pulled out his pipe and the Keeper shrugged, showing me again he'd locked up his mouth as he rolled his eyes.

Great – I was dealing with a group of children. No, children are more helpful than this.

Standing I walked across to Louise, sitting down on the coffee table in front of her, next to her now warm glass of lemonade.

"Grandma Louise..." I heard the Keeper snigger, repeating myself "Grandma Conrad. Was that Roger Conant?"

Chewing on her lip as she straightened out her tweed skirt, she nodded.

"...And was that John Dee's Grimoire he had under his arm?"

Louise sat motionless and just as I started to wonder if I needed to give her a shake, a deep furrow appeared between her eyes and across the length of her forehead. With a struggle she spoke,

"We believe so but..."

The Keeper interrupted "You believe so – I know so *Grandma*".

I turned, my index finger pointing just inches away from his face, prodding it in his face.

"Locked mouth remember? Silence", my voice rising.

He leant forward, snapped at my finger before, uttering an evil little laugh which bordered on the perverse, he slumped back.

Turning back to Louise she shuffled some more in her seat, smoothing her perfect skirt and re-crossing her legs. She knew what was coming and I could see she'd rather be anywhere else than being pushed to talking about this.

"So John Dee's Grimoire is this Voynich Manuscript? Or are they two different books?"

Griffin, the Keeper and Louise all looked up at me at exactly the same instant – the tension and worry written in lines each face, taught chins and hands balled into fists.

None of them spoke.

Spending a few seconds on each I waited for the

silence to be broken. After another minute I saw that no one was in a breaking mood.

With a voice that even sounded pissed and loud to my own ears I asked again,

"What is the Voynich Manuscript people?" I said trying not to screech but failing enormously.

Griffin cleared his throat and getting a nod from Louise and a furtive look from the Keeper, he stood as if it would help to be moving.

"We don't know but we do know they're two different books." Griffin said.

"That...at least...we do know." The Keeper grumbled "But as for what the Voynich Manuscript actually says – we've been able to work out elements but..."

"What? After all this you don't know? So who does?"

Shaking his head Griffin walked to the window, pulling back the curtains and peering outside. With his back still to me I heard his muffled voice answer,

"No one."

My mouth dropped open. Still holding the curtain he turned, meeting my eyes.

"No one" repeated Griffin. "Ever. That's just the problem".

Turning away I tried to digest it, I tried a different tact.

"So if you don't know what it is, why is it important?"

The Keeper spoke, his voice low and only just above a whisper, "Look Girly, there is no shortage of ideas. We have ideas up to our necks. What we need more of is facts." His eyes darted across the room, pleading. "Louise – for all the Gods, tell her."

Louise cleared her throat before she spoke, reminding me of Griffin. They have obviously spent too much time together.

"The Voynich manuscript is a document written around five hundred years ago. A member of our order, Ugo Boncompagni found the document and took it for safe keeping to Villa Mondragone in Italy and so we could decipher it. The order has spent lifetimes trying to unlock the secrets of the Voynich manuscript."

I heard the Keeper grumble "too many" under his breath and was rewarded with a scowl from Louise.

"So why is this manuscript so important?" I asked and Griffin answered.

"It's a mysterious book written in a language no one has ever been able to read – it's no language we've ever seen before. Basically what it says, who wrote it and why, is a complete mystery. For hundreds of years it's been an enigma to all humanity."

The Keeper jumped down from the table, "if it had stayed that way we'd all have been better off..."

"But it didn't?" I asked, addressed my question to the Keeper, who seemed to know a lot more about this than he'd been willing to say.

"Remember John Dee? He was a mathematician – he had a Grimoire of spells and incantations...and embedded within its cover, a knife, where it clicked in place."

"The same spell book given to Roger Conant just before he executed Sir Walter Raleigh?"

The Keeper nodded. "The same. Anyway Dee wrote his Occult books in what he called the 'Adamical language' or 'Celestial Speech'. He was convinced he spoke with Angels in their own language – he also referred to it as the first God language and wrote books in the language. Others believed he was visited by Demons not angels...and they had played tricks on him..."

The penny dropped as the Keeper finished speaking.

"You think John Dee's Grimoire and his writings will unlock the Voynich Manuscript? What then?"

Standing just an arm's length away the Keeper stood quite still as he took a breath before answering.

"It will solve one of civilizations greatest puzzles but more than that – we've been able to determine Dee wasn't crazy – the spell book was written in God's first language. The language of Adam.

My breath caught in my throat as I swallowed, rasping out my next nervous question – "If not?"

He grinned, answering almost flippantly, "Oh that's easy – it's either written in God's first language or the Devil's. Even reading out loud the pieces we've been able to translate have had interesting consequences..."

I almost slapped my own forehead,

"Dammit. That's what's killing these girls and hunting me. One of you tried to read the manuscript and..."

"...and when it was read it opened a portal into the world."

My hands began to flex and itch, I had such an urge to yell and pound my fists on the table, to swear and throw the close at hand flower vase across the room.

"You knew." My eyes accusing Griffin and Louise, wanting to waggle my finger in their faces. "You pointed me towards Raul – suggesting it was a werewolf and all along you knew it was a demon. Why?"

Louise stood, walked over putting her hand on my shoulder.

"Yes we knew. One of our own was taken. This is not their world any longer – they survive by possessing a person of power. Like you..."

"Like Marjorie...and like me. But why imply Raul was involved." I said under my breath, wanting to accuse but without fully understanding why she had done it.

"He is involved. We don't know what role he plays in this, but he has appeared too often, too close to events surrounding the manuscript, Dee's Grimoire and the murders to not be involved. We don't know everything Dear..."

"Sir Walter spoke of it being the time when he experienced Ague. He told Conant to cut off his head before the Ague came upon him - What is ague?"

Louise's face lost a little color. "Ague is having chills, fevers, sweats – it means a sharp fever – many of the signs of an oncoming possession that would be a likely consequence of using Dee's Grimoire without having the necessary safety precautions in place."

"So Roger Conant could have been equally possessed if he used John Dee's book?"

Louise pulled her cardigan tight around herself as she perched on the edge of the coffee table sitting her knees knocking against mine.

"We don't know but we do know the Grimoire is a focus of dark power – it was possibly the catalyst that caused the rise of black witchcraft within Salem. Wherever Dee's Grimoire has turned up its done nothing but cause death. Adamical language or not, it's plagued the world with nothing but misery. That's why we took it and why it's held here – with the Keeper."

I looked over at the small little man, a Dwarf that would have been perfect in a fantasy novel, the obvious ability to create illusion that passed for reality at will, he also had arms as thick as the trunks of my legs bunched cords running throughout. If his legs were anything like his arms, and I suspected if anything, they were significantly stronger, then he could pull me apart like a chicken wishbone.

"What are you looking at? Want to buy a ticket?" He said growling at me.

He was right – staring was rude but rude seemed to be his middle name. Hell, for all I know it's his first name as he sure as hell wasn't born a 'Keeper'. But with a cheesy smile I held his eyes. I needed help and friends right now if there was a demon out there looking to use my power and my skin as a new overcoat, but I wasn't going to back down from a staring contest with anyone.

He gave me the same cheesy grin back, locking his eyes on mine as we settled down to stare each other out without blinking.

With a scuff upside the back of both of our heads Louise interrupted our battle of wills with her usual stern tone.

"Stop playing with the children Keeper. It's late and we're staying. Tell us where we sleep. Sam, set a ward around the house so we don't get disturbed. I'm sure the Keeper has more than enough but extra won't hurt..."

With a sulk the Keeper broke from our contest and scuffed his feet along the floor swinging his arms in anger. "Who are you calling Dwarf old Lady – four or five hundred years ago you'd have gotten away with it but not today. Times have changed for the better Grandma..." He said grumbling.

I sat scratching my head, it didn't go unnoticed.

"What?" Louise rolled her eyes. "Don't tell me Nana didn't teach you how to set a ward? What was that women thinking? You're closer to being a necromancer than you are a true witch...stretch out your sense and do this..." She said.

With a tut, she made a gesture and I instantly felt the air re-aligning, Louise reaching out and take a hold of the air around the house, as she did she passed pieces of her will throughout like fairy lights strung together and as the willed particles touched their unwilled counterparts they joined. A giant linked bracelet of energy surrounded the house bound to her awareness – an extension of herself.

Having felt her create the ward, it made my mind flip that it hadn't occurred to me before. But I recognized it was the power within me which understood the lesson rather than my mind or spirit.

I instantly understood the sense of it rather than its mechanics.

But I couldn't even begin to understand how the Keeper had been able to create, un-create and recreate the homes I'd been sitting in, drinking a cool imaginary lemonade that satisfied my thirst. Now that was a lesson I'd like to learn.

As if reading my mind the Keeper walked past on his way out of room. He touched his nose as if telling me a secret he whispered,

"It was the Gnomes..."

Walking behind him hoping that he would eventually lead me to a place to freshen up, call my Dad then sleep I wondered what that meant. Gnomes? Was he kidding?

      The Keeper stopped and turned back,

      "No I'm not kidding". He said to my unasked question and continued out. I followed picking my chin off the floor.

Chapter 37

Putting the phone down on my Father I felt guilty. It's true I told him a few half-truths but they were not outright lies...I was staying with friends, that was the truth. Louise was a girl – of sorts – and I'm sure even Griffin went to a High school once upon a time... like I said...half-truths. Blowing my fringe vertical from my forehead, I looked around the bedroom, wondering what the next step was.

The summer flowered curtains were closed but I didn't need to be told there was darkness outside...I could lie back and admire the pretty flowers, tell myself all was peachy but I knew a malevolent creature was out hunting down women with power and murdering them on the other side. It had dominated me in my own mindscape, taunting me and was looking for me even as I sat in this perfect bedroom.

I turned the lock on the bedroom door, flicked off the light and lay back in the crisp cotton not bothering to undress.

Without being conscious of my breath slowing I fell asleep.

Chapter 38

My breath quickened and I was awake. A vibration beginning at my back teeth demanded I open my mouth and stretch it with the world's largest yawn. It intensified into a throb, which became a jangle and strangely transferred itself into the real world, my door shuddering with brisk knocks. Loud enough to make sure I'd awaken, quiet enough to let the rest of the house sleep.

I stood with my face a few inches from the wood of the door and did my best to hear through it. Nothing.

Leaning my face against its surface, I jumped as the person on the other side hit the door a few more times, knuckles strong and insistent.

Cursing I summoned up my courage and turned the lock on the door. It swung inwards, jamming against my toes. I stepped back turning on the bedroom light. Louise stood outside my door reaching a hand around the doorframe and turned off the light with a hiss.

"Do you want them to know we're awake?" She said, her voice a knife that cut through my night time half asleep confusion even though it wouldn't have registered above a whisper on the volume scale.

Trying to get my night vision back I stretched my eyes open wider and moved up closer to her.

"Who? Who's here?" I asked.

"Tell me you felt the ward activating? You were part of its creation, it should have warned both of us..."

"Ah...that would be the teeth ache, the vibration...the jangling thing?"

"No – that was the cell phone tower beside the house microwaving your brain – of course it was the ward...my goodness, remind me to take you through the basics...and I mean the basics, if we get back to Salem in one piece. Do you think you can do that?" Louise said, the image of a human shaped cactus in the desert materializing in my mind for absolutely no reason whatsoever.

Would it be wrong to beat the living daylights out of a women three times my age? Surely that was what the martial arts training was all about right? Damn...I knew the answer but the temptation was significant?

"Back to my first question...who's here?" trying not to make it obvious I was clenching my teeth.

"Are you being snippy with me young lady?" She growled in the darkness.

I may as well have placed an ad, nothing got past this woman. "I'm pretty sure we don't have time for this. Whoever triggered your ward did it three or four minutes ago. They could already be..."

A slice of a second later a shadow reached up to the ceiling in the hallway behind Louise. I bit down on my lip as I watched the shadow thin and extend, pointed fingers, a chin and nose that would have made the wicked witch of the west envious – if the shadow cackled, rubbed its hands together and talked of ruby slippers in the darkness, I wouldn't have been surprised.

As the creature turned the corner the shadow reached across the ceiling, I tracked it back to the body creating the inky stretched vision dominating the hallway.

And there he was...

Walking around the corner - the Keeper. A white and blue stripped soft and droopy cotton night cap perched on top but trailed all the way down his back. He shuffled in pointed slippers, tiny multicolored silk bows tied into his beard. Seeing the bows I tried to hold in a stomach twisting laugh, a small amount of it escaping as a giggle.

He shuffled down the hall, a candlestick in one hand, the other wiping sleep from both eyes. A yellow toothed yawn gave me a glimpse of dangling pink at the back of his cavernous mouth.

"What's up? Is there a problem?" He said before yawing wide and loud all over again.

Louise, in men's pajama's, stood, hand on her hip,

"Our ward was set off about five minutes ago. I had pushed the ring out a good distance but they could arrive at any moment..."

Despite looking like a whimsical nursery rhyme character in that sleeping get up, there was no mistaking resolution as he came instantly awake.

His eyes focused on the challenge of the soon to be invaders, chin jutting while his ham sized arms tensed and un-tensed. All of a sudden, I was glad to be on the side of the good guys.

I could see him calculating and planning to protect and defend, and I knew by the way my senses prickled he was ready to do so with extreme physical and magical prejudice.

"Where's Griffin?" I asked looking around for the last of the team.

With a smile a cheetah might give before it rips the throat out of a stray gazelle, the Keeper placed a finger on his lips.

"Let him sleep. We can deal with this...I'm not sure he would be that much use unless there's something about him you're not telling me..." giving me a slightly lopsided grin.

Louise brushed past him as she made her way quietly down the hall, bare feet on varnished wooden floorboards towards the stain glassed window.

Closing his eyes, the Keeper concentrated, his forehead stretched and white, the night cap pulled tight just above his thick bushy eyebrows. He swayed to the left and right, a partially heard word and motion made, I felt his will and spirit venture out.

Those senses of mine that were still embedded and entwined in the ward Louise and I had made, shied away from contact with the Keeper without any rationale. Even so I felt his mind testing and probing the ward, like he was tapping it with a mental hammer to see where it still held and where it was fractured.

Seemingly satisfied, I felt him pull back, his closed eyelids fluttering and as his mind disengaged, it briefly touched mine and in that moment I sensed his power, his conviction and more, his hunger.

It pulsed through him.

The coin of life in my pocket began to vibrate like an old fashioned alarm clock going nuts. My hand slapped down. Glancing up it was already too late, the Keeper's eyes fully opened, onyx passing across, making them completely black as he grinned, the cat that had, or would soon, eat the sparrow.

Stepping back, my heel caught on the carpets edge. Throwing my hand out I grabbed trying to stop my fall. With my usual perfect coordination, my hand pushed rather than grasped the door handle, failing to stop my descent.

The Keeper moved towards me.

Over his shoulder Louise leant out the window, peering at the ground below.

Giving Louise a fleeting look, he sped up his steps, grinning. I tried to get of his path but it was all I could do to stay upright.

As he ran forward, stretching to take a hold of my throat, I found my voice. Screaming "Louise" his iron trap fingers enclosed my windpipe.

My warning seemed unnecessary – Louise was already turning, her hand raised to strike. But almost unbelievably her steps slowed, pulling back from casting a spell.

She was hesitating because of me that had to stop. With my throat being squeezed, I reached out with my mind. A mental grenade instantly exploded in my head, almost knocking me senseless. I threw up the best wall of will that I could, a shock wave struck. A piercing headache hit me between the eyes as I staggered under his strength.

It was the clumsy stagger that saved me, his hand grasped further but came up clutching air. I guess most witches would have tried some incantations, some Hubble bubble toil and trouble or curse but being a navy brat with a fair share of scraps in tough schools under my belt, as he reached I kicked.

Even though my ears were ringing from his

mental slapping, my foot flew with a bone cracking thud, connecting between his legs. I fell back dazed but happy until the back of my head rapped hard on the floorboards, sending stars spinning across my vision.

Letting out a sound somewhere between an animal yell and a groan, the Keeper's weight landed on me even as I tried to roll away – but suffering with a migraine from hell and eyes refusing to focus. The Keepers was punching and screaming – all magic and spells forgotten as being kicked in the groin pushed logical thoughts from his head.

It's not every day that you get to see a dwarf go ape and start frothing at the mouth as he tries to punch and tear you apart but it's not even remotely amusing when you are the one underneath the onslaught. He was fierce.

He landed a full knuckle punch on the corner of my mouth, with a head snapping jolt, blood bursting into the back of my throat, my lip split. Turning my head, I got another punch on the side of my head for my trouble, my ear burning as his mallet fist struck hard, sending more church bells through my head.

The years of sparing helped as I brought my elbow around, with a twist, it sliced across the side of his head, partially dislodging him. Unfortunately his legs were tight around my waist, knees in deep.

Hearing someone running I tried to lift my head from the floor but it refused. Looking around him, I saw Louise running towards us –as the Keeper lost all control, his fists slamming down across my head, shoulder and chest.

Perhaps it was my noticing Louise or maybe he heard her but thrusting a hand across my throat he turned, mumbled and with one hand raised –flicked his wrist.

Louise flew, her body reversing direction. With a sickly crunch she hit the window at the back of the hall, elbows cracking against the window frame and almost flying straight through, glass smashing all around her.

Falling to the floor, shards of glass rained down.

Louise twitched, then lay still, gray hair splayed, covering her face, blood spreading through the gray strands and pooling shiny and bright around her head.

With a howl the Keeper turned back to me, his hand still across my throat, his weight pushing down. Hearing and feeling a crack.

Fear shot adrenaline straight into my bloodstream, like a syringe to the heart, making me frantic as both my hands ground his wrist bones, demanding he release his hold on my throat and give me air.

It didn't work. His forearm was cord tight and desperately strong.

With what felt like the last of my strength, I croaked out one word,

"Why?"

And with that he slightly slackened his hold, a trickle of air reaching my lungs. My lungs were almost euphoric.

"Why?" The Keeper asked, a bemused look on his face.

I nodded, not trusting myself to speak again in case he changed his mind and went back to choking. Resting on my abdomen, he kept his fingers pressing and bruising into my neck.

"Do you know how long I have been the Order's Keeper?" He said leaning forward, knees digging beneath my armpits, his eyes burning.

"Since even before your Father was born. I have been the Keeper for generations. My own kind long since passed from this world...only I remain, my never ending task, protecting and hold safe the orders treasures. What started as an honor became a curse. I'm tired. Do you understand?" his voice reaching out to a part of me that felt his suffering.

His words rocked me. Was this a task or multiple life sentences? What did he do to deserve such treatment? It was a curse.

We all dream of living forever and never truly consider the cost – to see all those you love and cherish suffer and die. How many times did the Keeper experience that loss before it became too much? Before it broke a part of him.

I met his eyes.

"You want to die? Is that it?" I asked, my body completely still.

He seemed to consider it then laughed as if it was the most absurd question he'd ever heard.

A small giggle popped from between his lips, "Why would I want to die? I've been made a promise...and he'll keep his promise. I know it."

What the hell was that supposed to mean?

As if reading my thought he lifted a finger to his lips to silence me.

"I was the Keeper but it called to me. After all those years of watching over it...of having it whisper to me. It never stopped. Whispering. Every second. Even when I slept. And it showed me the way. Those few words spoken from the Great Book ...he was released, allowed back into our world for a certain time each night where he belongs...when we translate more, he'll make the earth his true dominion, for all of time..." his eyes darting like a ferret in every direction, before scratching some unseen irritation in the crook of his arm, he took his hand away from my neck.

Reacting without taking the time to consider exactly what I was doing, I brought my fist up off the floor and into the side of his head, rolling as I struck.

He responded almost as quickly, knees squeezing together, refusing to give up his place, a bright trickle of blood running out his ear, between his hairy fingers held to the side of his head.

With a growl he put his face inches from mine, his beard tickling against my neck, his breath sweetly rancid.

"I've had enough of playing" he said, spitting out the words as he waved a hand, the room around us changing from teenage girl bedroom to evil kidnapping Dwarf décor – back to the original dark stone psycho gothic we had seen as we'd first walked towards the house. He'd given us a hint and we'd failed to notice.

I heard clicking, becoming a droning hum.

From the side of my peripheral vision I saw movement.

The Keeper's face cracked a sick grin as I turned my head to see the source of the weird clicking, like thousands of dried sticks falling to the wood floor.

Out of the iron grill at the base of the stone blocked wall, they erupted, spilling and flowing, pincers, stingers and insect limbs rolled and slid. The first few hundred worked to right themselves as their later brethren pushed and struggled. The front rows stabilized and I watched, wide eyed as they moved as one towards me.

At that moment everything slowed, perhaps it was the adrenaline and fear cocktail or my brain going into overdrive but I felt like I had all the time in the world. I squinted to see the front row of creatures in the half light.

It was hard to grasp what I was seeing, their images slipping and sliding inside my head, resisting being held and categorized. The only thing that seemed to make any sense was that they were not creatures of any birth but of a warped mind. It wasn't that they were dark or black, it was as if they were a moving mass of holes in space and time, hard shining Obsidian shelled scorpions as large as my hand, steroid enhanced snapping pincers, moving across the floor in a way that my mind couldn't translate it, threatened to blue screen, close down and wait for a reboot that hopefully wouldn't arrive.

Expecting six legs on each body running towards my head as the Keeper sat firmly down, body my skin crawled as I realized these abominations weren't moving like they should. These creatures weren't scorpions – a sick entity had spliced together the most vicious genetics of a scorpion and a viper. Their legs replaced by the rasping undulation of a serpent body. Chitinous plates of the scorpion's armor were attached to a sideways creeping viper, a single stinger and florescent green poison dripping fangs.

The Keeper smirked.

"Aren't they beautiful?" his voice a mixture of syrup and hysteria.

At this point answering was unnecessary and it was probably rhetorical anyhow... to me they looked like demonic extrusion. They were insectoid black, designed to cause as much pain and suffering as possible, they were light years from beautiful.

If there were any doubts before, the jury had come back in, and it was unanimous...the Keeper was officially insane.

Leaning forward his beard encircled lips pressing against my ear, tickling me as he talked.

"I bet you're wondering how long it will take you to die if even one of my master's creatures stings you?"

OK. It's one thing to be a crazed evil Son of a Dwarf serving a demonic master and threatening me with bastardized creatures from the abyss. That I can handle. Just.

But tickling me with his beard that pissed me.

I hated that more than anything. My grandfather would rub his stubble up and down my cheek knowing it freaked me out. Having this guy's goatee against my skin while he whispered sweet nothings about my imminent death was exactly that sensation. Damned annoying and quite creepy.

With a triumphant twitch of his mouth he sat back on my stomach, waiting for me to join him in conversation. Well the 'entertain the crazy person' hour had just ended so rather than encouraging him I lay back, keeping my mouth firmly shut.

Closing my eyes I considered placing my consciousness in a box and closing the lid until all of this was over. The tranquility I'd achieve using the mental and breathing techniques Nana Tobbot had me practice would be a perfect way to let all of this just cease to be important. But that would be quitting.

Driving his knees into my side, I gasped trying to resist reacting. He did it again, giggling before he answered his own question.

"Good of you to ask – well I'll tell you." his knees grinding ribs, cracking them.

"How long will it take you to die if one of these beauties kiss you?" His hand came across and slapped as I refused to join him in psycho conversation.

Careful not to show any pain, I turned my head until it was face up again. Ignoring my valiant refusal to respond for the insignificant showing of resistance that it was, he continued talking to himself.

"How long you ask?" He grinned. "Well, I'll tell you. You won't die, isn't that great? The poison reacts with your essence and they suck the life force... out of you. They're like cute little portals to the next dimension. As they feed, your soul is drained. That is what my master wants – yes he wants your death but more importantly you're necessary to give him more substance. Aren't you glad you asked? Isn't it a noble use of your life?"

I couldn't take anymore. If I was going to die then better to not die listening to his ranting and having his damned hair tickling.

Opening angry eyes I spat up at him,

"I didn't freaking ask. Can you just get on with the gloating and the killing part already? I haven't got all day you know. I have things to do, angels to meet..."

And as if I'd never spoken at all I lay back, relaxed, taking a nice deep breath, the back of my head against the floor.

I should really look for my center, to gain some balance and tranquility. Tranquility my rear end...

With a yell I sat up, the top of my head aiming for his face. The pleasure of the next few moments spanned multiple senses as I heard and felt his nose crack from the force of my skull hitting him right on the bridge of the nose. Or 'on the button' as they say in the gym. I had to admit it, it felt good, really good. It shouldn't but sorry, it did. Blood splashed, running down my face and into my grinning mouth – tangy.

I allowed myself a smile. All lies – I grinned like I was eating a banana sideways.

Rocked backwards, his hand across his face, the nose bleed gushed between his fingers.

Flicking a look to the side the scorpion snakes had gained while we'd struggled. The noise of thousands of pincers clacking intense as their serpent bodies rasped across the stone floor in a wave of writhing antimatter.

This was the last chance I'd get before they were within striking distance, I had no clear strategy for rescuing myself and saving the day and I had only a few seconds to come up with one. Nope. Blank. Back to Navy brat force...

Throwing up a knee, lifting my hips off the ground with a jerk and bucking with every ounce of energy I had left. With his hands still held across what I hoped was a broken nose the Keeper had made the mistake of relaxing his knees on my sides. Bucking again, I grabbed his upper arms and pulled, frustration and pure blinding fear giving me the added spice I needed.

With a snot and blood muffled yell he flew over my head and gaining air landed hands and knees first in the swarm of his master's creatures.

As I turned onto my own hands and knees I came face to face with the front row of creatures. Swallowing I waited for the first poison tipped strike to send me on my way.

Their burning red eyes drilled into my vision as I tensed.

Then the tide turned.

The Keeper scrabbled, his nails scratching tracks in the wooden floor with his blood encrusted hands, trying to push himself to his feet as the killing machines responded to his blood and warmth, a wave of scalpel sharp claws slicing and gouging, poison dripping stingers flicking and sticking.

White faced I tried not to puke as I watched the Keeper, his eyes wide and disbelieving as his Master's mindless death machines washed over him, thousands of bleeding cuts erupting across his face, neck, hands, all visible flesh turned red as his skin disintegrated. After piercing his skin, they burrowed deeper, muscle from bone, finger tips transformed to finger bones, the flexor muscles of his forearm cut and pulled back.

As I pushed myself back, my butt sliding, I watched his extremities being consumed. His eyes never letting me free required to watch his face bleached white with intense pain. Red froth and green spittle formed at the corners of his mouth, the toxins running rampant through every fiber.

Watching his slow dismemberment I recalled what he'd whispered, beard tickling my ear. He had gloated their sting wouldn't kill, but would suck the life force from me. The Keeper had tauntingly assured me they were his Master's syringes, designed to use my essence to his master. To make me a part of his master, giving him more substance in this world.

He was wrong.

His Master's warped creations were his essence but the pooling slick of blood and offal surrounding his increasingly stripped down body, said he was dying. Unless he was a good at faking it, he was so close to death he'd be on the elevator down and would be holding a pitchfork at any moment.

The keeper had been wrong, very wrong, and was paying the price.

They dove into his chest, all the while snipping and stinging. With a gurgle he looked over at me, his mouth moving soundlessly trying to form words that wouldn't come. With pleading eyes he shook his head de, his mouth opening wide, black scorpion snakes erupting from it like solid black vomit.

It was at that ghastly moment that he spoke to me, as he crossed from living to death, his words appearing strangely quiet and peaceful in my mind.

Light disappeared, plunging all the Keeper had created into darkness –his voice reverberating throughout the house.

"I pass on the burden. You are my Heir child. Use it better than I. Now if you have any humanity, for pity sake kill me.' His last message as he balanced between life and death, tipping over.

His heir? Time enough later, hopefully...

Judging from the slicing creatures flowing in and through him, his death was a certainty before I could do more than blink.

I took a step forward to help, a row of scorpion snakes pulled away rearing up in response. Before I could make a decision, the keeper bit down on the slippery Exoskeleton of the scorpion snake in his puss ridden mouth. Winking at me, he chuckled, sliding into the mass of razor edges, the coin in my pocket burning into my leg. He gave his last choking gasp, the Keeper of the Order of the Dragon died at that moment.

A release of energy hit me, making my body tingle and shiver, the image of a bag of microwave popcorn filling up its bag then the ping of being done appeared involuntarily in my head. Then the Keeper replaced it, a nod of recognition with his trademark sardonic smile. With a breath of cold air from nowhere ruffling my short hair and making me close my eyes for a moment, I was finally left alone, my own salty sweat dripping and running into my eyes.

I pushed the Keeper's passing away, filing it to consider later, assuming I had a later.

The creatures closest to the keeper's diminutive skeleton paused, finished with their first murder. As one they all stopped, waiting for the next set of instructions. They didn't take long to arrive. Red smoldering eyes turned my way.

Chapter 39

That was the jolt that got my brain and my feet functioning again. Groaning, I did my best to stand. Pincers waved at their next target.

Trying to pull myself up my ribs complained at be asked to move after the beating the Keeper had given me, I wiped the blood seeping from my lips and nose on the back of my hand.

Standing, I cursed as my boots failed to get a good grip, the Keeper's blood and worse making the stone floor impossibly slick. My wrist popped and twisted as I fell back to the floor.

"Shit" I said, the first set of creatures two inches at most from striking at my leather boots. They stood up on back legs, pincers snipping at the air, their stingers arching and readying to slash down and embed their poisoned tips into my flesh.

Refusing to whimper, I pulled my feet up to my chest and tried to push myself up, my wrist buckling as the scorpion snakes slide forward. Was this it?

The Keeper sat up, one eyeball dangling. Raising a hand I wasn't sure if he was gesturing or waving goodbye but by the looks of the scorpion snakes I wouldn't have time to worry about it. I watched as, with a last twitch, he fell back into the unholy morass of swirling twitching bodies.

As the last elements of the Keepers will were sucked from his body, the husk that remained slid into the insect-reptilian morass.

With a groan, deep gashes appeared across every surface. The house he had created shook and complained like it too was dying; walls, floor and ceilings rupturing.

The creatures gripped the stone floor and despite the earthquake like vibrations worked to move closer. With a wrench and a crack like the heavens were bursting, the floor split, tilting downwards. A deepening crack appeared, and with a lurch the floor tipped steeper still a creating a dust ridden slide. Gaining momentum I slid closer towards the creatures which had inched forward despite being perched on a surface tilting at a 45 degree angle. One of the many benefit of a snakes skin I guess, I wasn't so lucky.

Scuffing my boots against the increasingly steep dusty floor as I scrabbled for grip, desperate to get some grip as I slipped without any hold to stop myself.

Yelling I edged closer, my fingers clawing frantically as the ground tipped down further. The only reason why I was not being stung and sliced into pepperoni was even the scorpion snakes were losing their grips. I watched as the back layer and the remnants of the keeper, fall through the widening gash in the wall, my raw fingers trying to tighten my hold on the dusty floor.

I doubted the impact of falling from the second floor would kill me – it would be the landing on the pile of irate and hungry scorpion snakes that might do the trick.

Intensifying my efforts I turned and made a desperate push to get back up to the edge of the slab I was suspended on, my fingertips stretching up to reach while kicking at the scorpion snakes that had somehow managed to stay attached and were moving closer.

With a crack the slab jolted and tipped to an even more precarious angle, my toes, without any real grip, lost the battle.

Biting down in determination I made a last desperate effort, pumping my feet, the tips of my toes running over and over against the now vertical stone. A black writhing mass of creatures were fully visible on the ground one floor down.

I sprang, stretching and screaming, the end of my fingertips managing to hang over the edge of the near vertical slab. Glancing below, I mentally high fived as the last row of creatures fell to land unharmed to the ground below. As I did, the few fingers that held me began to loosen.

There was no way I could hold my body weight for

more than a few more seconds. Then I'd be joining the Keeper's body down below.

With closed eyes I strained, willing my strength to hold me for hours but knowing that I had seconds at best. My teeth ached as I kept my jaw locked straining.

A smell of tobacco and aftershave clouded over me.

Mr. Griffin's face appeared floating above, a grim look passing across his straining face as he clasped onto my arms.

Grunting, he pulled, inching me slowly upwards a sheen of sweat appearing across his forehead, unfortunately it wasn't limited to there, clammy hands slipped along my arms until they arrived on each of my wrists. My breath tightened in my chest as I realized he may not be able to pull me up, this may not be the happy ending I had expected seeing his face poking at from the ledge above.

What happened to challenges, nightmares and even pain but happy endings in the end? Then I remembered the Keeper's face, the feeling of being invaded, the heat that washed over and through me as he died. The husk of his sucked dry body reinforced what I hadn't realized before – some endings are not happy, they're bone achingly sad...and scary.

Looking up into Griffin's eyes I saw determination then it dawned on me that he wasn't going to be enough. He leaned over the edge, trying to get more leverage. My weight pulling him over as he refused to let me go.

I knew then that I was going to keep slipping, and worse, the more Griffin refused to give up, the greater the chance I'd take him with me. Then we'd both fall into the seething mass and they'd consume both of us in seconds.

So much for my happy ending.

Griffin grunted as he managed to move me in the right direction. Gaining a few inches we both cursed as my hands slid further through his sweating fingers. He shuffled even further forward, somehow managing to keep hold of me while most of his body was over the edge.

I could see icy determination in his eyes but as he strained, I dangled, swinging as he began to lose his own balance, tipping precariously over the edge.

That was enough. Griffin had tried his best but I wasn't going to go into the afterlife with his death on my conscience.

Giving him a smile of reassurance.

I let go.

Chapter 40

My fingers opened. I'd let go, no longer holding on desperately to his wrists.

Griffin growled through clenched teeth, eyes shocked,

"You're...not...going to...fall. I won't...let...you."

"You have too." my voice calmer than I felt, sounding resigned, even to my own ears. "Don't worry, it won't take long."

Shaking his head his moist hands pulled harder, squeezing my thin wrists close to breaking.

"I'm not taking you with me..." and began to kick against the slab, my body swinging out, making it near impossible for Griffin's already slippery hands.

His eyes narrowed as he strained, wavering, too close to the edge, starting to fall, his eyes jumping to look at the creature swarming below.

In that instant, I knew Griffin would rather fall with me than fail, letting me fall. Whether I liked it or not, he would sacrifice himself for me.

Having kicked out with my legs I had created the momentum that would drag us both over the edge. Sometimes I just screw up, other times my screw ups take on epic proportion – this was beyond epic.

We weren't alone. Four of us had come into this house. The Keeper was dead, that left Griffin, me and Louise. I'd seen her fly, the Keeper's slamming her almost through the window with a sickening thud.

My whole body winced at the pain she as she was knocked into unconscious oblivion. Unfortunately for Louise I needed her awake and right now. Closing my eyes, I stilled my body, my breath gently released from semi-opened lips.

I calmed my fear.

If Griffin could just hold on for a few more minutes...I needed to wake up Louise, we need two pairs of hands.

Chapter 41

Penetrating a person's mental defenses and entering their mind was a no-no.

One of the first lessons Nana taught was how to create barriers to stop unwanted visitors taking a joyride through the mental fun park that was my mind. It was the first and hardest lesson I'd learnt.

I needed to smash through Louise's resistance, find her subconscious and persuading it to wake up to world of hurt so she could pull my butt out of my current precarious position before Griffin and I both joined the creepy crawlies on the floor below.

Breaking through the defense of Louise's mind was both daunting and more than a little repulsive. It went against the fundamentals of being a good witch. Doing it while she slept, her body trying to repair itself was exactly the opposite of what she needed right now.

Sorry Louise - but I'd rather be around so you can be pissed at me face to face.

I pictured myself stepping back from my physical form, my consciousness split in two. Now this was the tough bit. I needed enough will and awareness to stay hanging from Griffin's hands, clasping onto his wrists while sending enough of myself out to locate Louise. Think of it like that head patting, tummy rubbing trick you learnt as a child. Pat your head, rub your tummy in a circle and oh yeah, recite every word in the dictionary and its full meaning and you're getting close to how difficult this was going to be.

Thankfully dangling above killer scorpion snakes, while dramatic, did not take a huge amount of brain power or thought aside from 'How the hell did I get myself into this mess? And I was used to thinking that particular sentence.

With a shudder I was floating above the ground, holding onto absolutely nothing and I wasn't falling. That was the clue that I was now not in my own body.

Looking back at myself I looked peaceful taking slow breaths with poor Griffin pink faced, jowls shaking and sweat dripping as he refused to release his white knuckled grip on my wrists. If I get out of this he's one guy who will be on my Christmas card list until I reach my one hundredth birthday.

No time to enjoy the scenery.

I caught the glint from the small circular bald spot at the top of Griffin's head, behind him was the bedroom door.

Down the long hall, shoes were attached to stockinged feet, which lay slack and unmoving. Louise's upper body hidden behind a credenza that ran along the wall.

Picturing myself at the end of the hallway, a thought later I was floating above Louise's unconscious form. If I had a stomach to feel it sinking this would have been the moment when it would have fallen into my boots.

There were a few stand out obvious facts - the jagged bone was splintering out the side of her neck which scared the hell out of me and if that wasn't enough even I knew Louise's head should not be pointing in that direction. You could teach your body to get into some pretty extreme positions but I was pretty sure 'one hundred and eighty degree rotated head' was not a move you'd see anytime soon in a Yoga show manual until humankind goes through a few more evolutionary cycles.

Much as Louise intimidated me, her death made even this shadow of myself sick with sadness. Pulling my eyes away from her twisted neck, the white bone mocking my attempt to resuscitate her. I glanced down the rest of her body.

This couldn't be.

As her broken body lay looking like a smashed spoilt child's doll, I saw it, her chest rose. Louise still breathed.

I knew Louise had a force of character that made Genghis Khan seem meek and mild but this was just plain freaky. Pulling more energy from my physical body still suspended about the hole, I prayed I wouldn't be draining it to the point of releasing my hold on Griffin's arms. If the lights went out and I found myself being dragged into the next world I'd know I pushed it too far.

I willed the thought of myself into the space her fractured body occupied.

My spirit form slammed against the energy Louise's subconscious had erected. The thought of being inside her body when she was so close to death made my teeth chatter in fright. She could be waving a big hello and how-ya-doing' to ancestors as I took up residence in her physical form. If that happened it wouldn't improve my chances of getting to the prom.

Nana Tobbot had reluctantly explained the mechanics of what I was attempting to do, even though she had her doubts about giving me that knowledge. Having made a decision to explain, she had been as thorough as ever.

Water can pass through plant membrane, what I was trying to do with Louise was not completely dissimilar but the energy and resistance was an order of magnitude greater. Tough, I had no choice, I needed Louise awake. There was also a chance that even though Louise could check out her own butt if she were able to open her eyes – I might be able to bring her back from the edges of death from inside her.

I willed myself forward, expecting the molasses resistance I'd felt once before when Nana had allowed me to try.

With Louise, it was like knocking against a layer of diamond with a feather duster. There was no way this was going to work. I'd tried but I was done.

I was going to die.

And just like that I had an idea.

The Keeper had spoken of an heir, the coin of life and death had vibrated, recognizing the Keeper's passing into the next place.

If Louise's broken neck was anything to go by, she should be there too, knowing her giving him a good tongue lashing and some slaps upside the head.

But she wasn't. She was still breathing. She was refusing to go quietly. Louise...was being difficult. Go figure.

The coin had not vibrated, she was still here. I just needed to find a way to get through to her, to drop her defenses enough for me to help her and me.

Reaching into my imagined pocket I pulled out the life and death coin, knowing the original was still swaying back and forth in my real body that had little time left.

I hoped the essence or the thought of the coin would be enough. There was no telling if the real coin would work, let alone my thought rendering of the coin.

Taking it in my palm I placed it against Louise's forehead, holding it still between her eyes.

Closing my own, I focused every ounce of energy I had left on that one focal point. I'd been taught to melt into the mind of another, to pass gradually like pouring water slowly into a container.

This was the opposite.

Straining I jabbed with my mind at the very point where I'd placed the coin. As I did it began to vibrate, to twist and turn, faster and faster and then like a drill boring through that diamond layer, I was inside Louise mind.

Chapter 42

I was standing in a place that made my teeth jangle.

If the sun could fill a room with whiteness so bright it would burn even the air away, it would only partially describe the energy of the place I was standing within. It was painful, I couldn't fathom why my spirit wasn't boiling and blistering and above it all a scream constant and terrible.

Putting hands to my ears I tried to drown out the noise but as they were not real hands and were not real ears my chances of success could be summarized as 'shit to none'. The scream went beyond noise and pushed through into motion – feeling like I was standing next to an epic sized speaker where her pain was noise was underpinned with thrumming sensation.

Her death defying scream penetrated my sanity. If I was a wine glass I'd have smashed from the vibrations.

I considered giving up, escaping back to the relief of dying among the scorpion snakes – it would be easier than dealing with this power and pain.

The problem was I wasn't a quitter. Creating the image of myself I tried to look through the brightness, to see some sense of depth and contour but the light was too intense. Raising a hand out in front of myself I stepped forward not feeling my way because there was nothing to feel.

I needed to find the core of Louise.

The best way to think about the mind is to imagine a maze of boxes, each self-contained and important to the owner in some way. Right now I was in one of the rooms on the periphery of Louise's mind and yet despite the distance, the screaming pain was rattling through this room too intensely for me to bare.

I needed to find a way to communicate with Louise, to have her hear me.

I stepped forward, tentatively, exploring.

With my second step I was swatted to the side, flying through nothing with the distinct sensation that I'd been hit by almost enough energy to crush me.

Adding a scream of my own I tried to get through to her.

"Wait. Louise wait. It's me. It's me. By all the spirits...Louise..."

She responded by pounding me from the opposite direction, sending me spinning the way I'd just come. Thankfully there were no walls inside her mind for me to be crushed against. A spirit couldn't be crushed in the spirit world could it? Damn, I never asked Nana that one. Imaginary Fingers crossed.

Taking a stand I stopped my sideways motion, planting my feet firmly on the white floor, no substance visible in any direction, I was literally standing in a featureless landscape with the sound of Louise's screaming pain pounding from every direction.

I needed to fight fire with fire. Concentrating I pulled every nightmarish, ghastly thought and feeling I had inside me. The fear washing through me since the murders, confronting the demon in my mindscape, failing, powerless and beaten. I wrapped in the Keeper's betrayal, his horrific death...my mother leaving me and my father alone. And when I thought that was enough Nana's death washed over me, the grief finally free; Marjorie's death...believe me, when it came to throwing out all the bile and gristle of my life I had enough to rival even Louise's screaming torment.

Louise was almost mindless with the pain her body was undergoing, even so, I needed....

Her....

...to....

hear...me....

And

she....agghhhhhhhhhHHHHHHHHHHHHHHHH....

...would...DAMMIT.

I released the crap of a lifetime like a thunderclap of negativity and sent it echoing through the maze of Louise's mind.

Chapter 43

Dammit, Dammit...Dam...

Silence.

It was so silent it almost made me stumble over the nothingness at my feet.

Imagine a completely quiet place and a gun suddenly and unexpectedly goes off with an enormous clap of noise.

This was exactly the same in reverse.

White silence.

"Louise" I said my whisper sounding like a shot, scared I was giving her an excuse to start screaming again.

Nothing...

"Louise...It's me...Sam. Sam Ray."

I heard the footsteps coming closer.

As if she turned a non-existent corner, a women, about my age, with long brown hair in a wholesome 1950's cut appeared.

I watched her in skirt and blouse like she was walking after a leisurely country walk look around, checking the floor as if she were looking for something she'd lost, confused.

She hadn't noticed me. I was sure it was Louise or at least how Louise saw herself. Young, vibrant, strong with a big dose of English country.

I felt an urgency, the fact my body was literally slipping through Griffin's sweaty fingers made me want to grab her by the shoulders. But the expression of loss on her face made me hesitate.

Walking forward I put my hand on her shoulder.

Pulling her eyes up from the floor like she was afraid by doing so she lose whatever she desperately needed to find, we looked into each other's eyes.

Like an icicle thrust into the roof of my mouth I touched her pain.

It was arctic cold and blinding.

What made me think the challenges of my life could come close to those Louise had experienced. This was too much for her, I had no right. Letting my hand fall I began to close my eyes, starting to will myself out of Louise's mind and back to my own body.

A gentle weight touched my shoulder stopping me from making the jump. The young women's face glowing with a wide and happy smile.

"It's OK Sam." She said. "Don't worry, it will be OK." She brought her other hand up to match the first before she pulled me into an embrace, her lips against my earlobe.

"It's OK Sam. I can bare the pain. I have for years already. But what I couldn't bare would be to die knowing I could have saved you and didn't."

Stepping back her smile faltered and flickered as her eyes went back to the ground and for a moment I thought I was going to lose her again.

But with a strength of will she lifted her eyes back to mine, the smile gone as she faced what we needed to do together and fast. Neither of us welcoming what was to come, we had no choice.

"I'm going to lower the barriers to the center of my being." She whispered. "You can take control but..." Her face paled before she could say the rest of the sentence.

I finished it for her.

"But when I do I'll experience every memory, every pain and every feeling you have."

Nodding she brushed the long hair away from her face with her hand, a nervous gesture I'd never noticed old Louise making.

"I've lived with it for so long." Louise the younger said.

I hoped I could cope with it for the time it would take to pull me free of the pit.

"Now" I said squeezing my eyes shut bracing myself.

Chapter 44

The solid ball of pain hit me like being kicked in the guts by a steel toe capped boot. Those sensations just the appetizer to the searing pain of my neck, feeling the rip, the bones fragmented point jutting through the bleeding gash on Louise's neck.

Hell. No wonder I was hit by her constant scream as soon as I'd entered her mind, living or more accurately, dying, with this kind of pain would have already driven me crazy.

Fully lowering her control I found my spirit form rushing through every part of Louise's mind like water rushing through the maze all at once. Multiple instances of myself appeared at every point within her mind. Every image, smell and feeling she'd saved through her life. Her memories radiated through me as I soaked up every lesson, fear and joy she'd ever had.

Taking control of her mind I opened my mouth and pumped out all the anger and pain, feeling like I would never stop, constant agony.

There was no other way to cope.

Fingers steepled, I pushed, sitting up. My legs were twisted in odd directions, brown leather shoes I'd never wear pointed east and west.

Taking a knee, I gave it a good tug feeling it snap, crackle and pop like rice crispies. With a yank, I found its socket, pain stabbing repeatedly until my teeth finished chewing up the agony. This was just the preparation for the real deal.

Louise's neck.

I didn't have time to hesitate. My real body could already be a second away from meeting those Scorpion snakes up close and personal and Griffin too. After all this suffering and torture for Louise, I sure as hell wasn't going to go without a fight.

Tensing my jaw I grabbed my neck with my left hand, my right going over the top of my head. Before it could do what was necessary, a crack appeared in the wall beside me, the disintegration moving more quickly sending up clouds of dust.

I was hoping this was going to be like clicking my neck with a quick jerk in the morning after sleeping funny. Yeah right.

Louise's neck was 180 degrees further around that Mother Nature had intended, if she had gas she'd definitely be the first person to know. I held my breath and with a spine grinding twist, I pointed Louise's head in the right direction. Needing to pass out more badly than at any time in my life, I ignored it focusing on the wound on her neck.

White pointed bone slivers bursting through a pomegranate red rupture. I focused on the binding broken bones together, controlling every fiber of Louise's body.

I concentrated on knitting them together, smoothing the splintered edges, then lastly, closed up the gash.

Pushing down an inhumanly strong and desperate need to pass out and let the darkness swallow us both, eyes closed I/Louise struggled to her knees, panting, head down, hair loose and cascading. I/we stopped there, trying to get some air into our lungs, gasping. Gritting our teeth, we stood. Louise was going to hurt when I left her but right now, she needed to help get my ass out of the pit.

Looking along the hallway the building slowly deteriorated around me. Fissures appeared on every surface, pieces of masonry falling to the floor below to crush scrabbling scorpion snakes. Well, at least there was a silver lining.

Staggering Louise's body forward we lurched through the bedroom door and stood swaying. I tried to take in how the floor had come away from the walls, one side on the ground below creating a near vertical giant slide, Griffin's legs visible and kicking. The rest of Griffin was invisible below the edge of the pit, his legs sliding, losing their ability to counterbalance his torso. Grunts came from over the lip of the hole.

Griffin gave a muffled yell of warning to the world as he came to the end of his ability to hold my physical self and just as I suspected, he kept fighting, even as we both toppled forward. He was being dragged in too.

Jumping, I grabbed at his feet as he disappeared. My old lady hands straining to keep a hold on, hoping his shoes wouldn't loosen, leaving me trapped inside Louise's body with a handful of men's tan comfortable shoes.

Digging Louise's wider than fashionable heels into the ground I bent at the knees, ignoring the fact that Louise's checkered brown skirt was riding up to her waist. Sitting back, I tried to scoot backwards, my butt scrapping along the concrete slab. With a slow but persistent pressure I strained. Louise steel inner strength rocked but I wanted my own body back and soon.

The first sign I was beginning to win the battle was seeing the back of Griffin's head but I couldn't let up, I needed to keep pulling until he could get some traction of his own. The two of us together should be able to get Sam up.

"Keep holding on Griffin. For goodness sake don't let her slip through your fingers now..."

He didn't answer, too busy trying to keep a hold. His voice croaked out.

"I...I can't hold on any longer. There's a crack on the slab's surface." He said. "Sam, your real body needs to use your toes to help. I don't have enough strength left to pull her up."

I swallowed. I was keeping Louise upright and functioning. But she was all that was keeping Griffin and my real body from falling to the writhing creatures below. If I went back to my own body and gave Louise control of hers, if she flinched or let go, even for a second, Griffin and I would be gone. Very gone.

As if reading my mind, Griffin spoke through gritted teeth.

"Trust her Sam. She's a game one. She won't even hesitate, not even for a second. We'll both be up and out of this in no time...I would bet everything on her, Sam."

I remembered the moment when I had truly occupied Louise's mind, knowing her perhaps better than she even knew herself. Louise wouldn't even blink but the pain she was going through, the body's need to slip into unconsciousness. Hells bells.

Whispering a small farewell I jumped out of Louise's mind and back into my own. Instantly grasping Griffin's wrists tighter and taking a quick shaky breath.

Feeling a jerk, my body lowered, gaining a slight swing as Louise hesitated, just for a nanosecond. Then she strained, and began pulling us up. Finding the crack in the fractured slab, I stuck my toes in and tried to relieve some of the weight while tightening my grip on Griffin's wrists, just in case.

Giving him some release from the constant weight that he'd been holding with my toes I waited for a second or two, hoping that would help him get some of his strength back.

With a nod, Louise audibly gasping from above, Griffin red cheeked and straining I was pulled up, legs kicking and scrabbling. They inched me upwards.

After maybe a hundred years, I crested the edge swinging a leg over, my knee a lever. With a twist and the largest exhale on the planet, I was back on solid ground, my heart beating out a drum solo beneath my leather suit as I lay looking up at the cracked ceiling above.

Chapter 45

It didn't take long for the euphoria of being alive to wear off to the point where anger could peek its red face into my thoughts and stick out its tongue at me. The ceiling looked the same, the scorpion snakes still clicked and clacked down below and if I looked over the edge, I'm sure I'd see the Keeper's smothered body.

My panting eased and I realized I was going to get another round in this fight after a near permanent knock out. I've heard when you have a near death experience your whole life flashes before your eyes, but it didn't happen like that for me. All I saw as part of my awareness held onto Griffin's arms, while the rest went off to take over Louise's body, were the last few days – over and over.

I had enough brainpower to think about three things.

Holding onto Griffin's wrists.

Keeping my real body breathing.

Every moment since the first murder on my doorstep. My subconscious had free reign with my conscious mind busy elsewhere and with that release it turned over each and every moment. Then there was the second girl's murder on Salem common. An unexplained connection to Raul. My mind being invaded. The Keeper's betrayal and death.

And like a person walking blindfolded through a hedge maze I found myself at the Science Advisor to Elizabeth I, a spell book and its linkages to the supposed ultimate book of power.

Considering the pain I and people I cared about had been through, I found myself at the end of that hedge maze with a significant case of "Severely Pissed".

This was war. The Keeper's master had better be all powerful otherwise I was going to kick him unfairly and squarely in the gonads, just like I had the keeper.

Chapter 46

Resolved, I rolled over onto my side. Louise was lying a few feet away, eyes closed, Griffin was leaning over her, tapping her cheek gently.

"Don't panic Mr. Griffin. She's going to be fine. Trust me, I know."

I watched his Adams apple twitch, then his concerned eyes were turned my way. I'd seen fear in those eyes myself as I hung from his arms, both of us ready to die but it was nothing compared to the fear that was in them now.

Turning back around he raised his hand to wake her.

With closed eyes her lips moved, a slight whisper.

Leaning in closer he quickly brought his ear so close her lips brushed against him.

"Say it again Louise. I didn't hear." He said, his voice quivering with desperation.

I watched her lick her lips, her tongue bringing moisture to dry cracked lips.

He moved closer still, afraid he'd miss her next few words.

"You slap me again old Man and I'll make you regret it every day for the next twenty years..."

He sat up, a broad grin lighting up his face, then moving down again, placed a delicate kiss on her cheek before he spoke into her ear.

"And I'll enjoy every minute of it, you Battle-axe."

She gave him a half serious slap on the face,

"That's for calling me a Battle Axe you old Fraud" and before she changed her mind pecked him back. "And that's for saving my life, you'll probably regret it tomorrow but it's too late now."

Griffin couldn't have been happier. Louise turned to me, holding out an arm.

I pulled her up and she dusted herself down as if she just got up from a picnic instead of having been thrown against the wall, having her neck broken and a strange seventeen year old girl running around inside her head. The only signs that she'd been in pain like you wouldn't believe were a few spots of perspiration across her forehead and her pale face.

You had to hand it to her, she was a feisty old bird.

Locking icy blue eyes on me and I saw something that hadn't been there before – if I wasn't a little lightheaded from my own near death experience I would have sworn it was a new found respect.

"What's do you think our next move should be Sam?" She said with a slight smile.

Well knock me over with a feather...

That was as close to a thank you as I could ever expect from Louise. Then, just as I was about to pinch myself she knocked me to the side three times in one hour.

"Thank you Sam." her elegant fingers reaching out to touch my shoulder and brushed them against my face. Stepping forward she took my face in both her hands. This was starting to feel just a little weird.

With my face between both her hands I looked from her to Griffin and back, the floor pitching and shaking like a storm in a gale as the walls continued to crumble.

"What?" I said, flicking a look between them.

Griffin placed his palm on my forehead.

Disregarding the fact that I was a human being standing right in front of him, he spoke directly to Louise.

"She's been through a lot. Her body's probably just overworked..."

Now I was starting to get just a bit nervous.

"What?" I said, raising my own hand to my head. I couldn't feel a thing. "What? I feel fine apart from not having slept for who knows how long?"

Shaking her head Louise took me by the shoulder and started to walk me out of the bedroom and into the hallway, ignoring the masonry falling in large clumps around us and sending up clouds of dust.

"It's not that you have a slight temperature. You are burning up, it's like you have been radiated if I didn't know better..."

I started to speak but she cut me off.

"No – this is no joke Sam. The Keeper's last words. Do you remember them?" She asked, Griffin stopped following us, his feet locked to the ground.

"What last words? What are you talking about Louise?"

Her eyebrows rose, questioning, perhaps doubting what she'd heard if Griffin hadn't heard it. But I'd heard it too. Moving her hands from my shoulder and letting it fall I said,

"He said I was his heir. It felt like I was a lean cuisine in a microwave, like I was being pumped with heart. It was weird."

Griffin and Louise shared a glance before Griffin, swallowing, walked between us, taking us both by the elbows.

"Well, temperature or no temperature. We have to get out of here and the old Keeper's master is still out there somewhere. We have to stop him, it or her before they kill again."

Digging in my heels I pulled, yanking my arm from his grasp.

"Hold it there hombre. What do you mean the 'old Keeper'? I hope you're not suggesting I'm the new Keeper?" my voice quivering as even the possibility nearly made me lose my breakfast, lunch and dinner I haven't even eaten, all at once.

Griffin looked down as he shuffled his feet. Louise tenderly but without room for any argument took my elbow and led me stiff but un-resistant along the corridor.

"Right now none of us are any the wiser about what the Keeper meant. But I do know that outside this house is a swarm of creatures that have already killed once this evening. I'd rather not give them the chance to do the same again."

She glanced at Griffin, "Griffin dear, come along. We don't have time for dilly dallying, we need to find a way out of this house. Now, if you could just take a quick peek downstairs..."

Protesting but happy with her treatment of him, the clearest example Louise was back on form, Griffin stood at the top of the stairs. As he prepared himself he closed the buttons on his tweed jacket, a brown leather elbow patch brushing the wall of the stairwell as he took tentative steps down, briefly looking back.

Griffin was either very brave or was more afraid of looking bad in front of Louise than the Demonic creations that were likely at the bottom of the stairs.

I don't know much about the animal kingdom but I'm guessing snakes, even Scorpion snakes have a bit of a tough time with staircases. Griffin could find the room below carpeted with creatures waiting for us to try to leave as the house crumbled around our ears.

Holding my breath I waited for Griffin to come back or to hear sounds telling us he wouldn't be...

Chapter 47

Griffin's round pink face appeared from around the corner of the stairwell, eyes downcast and worried.

"Well?" I asked beating Louise to the punch, her lips half open, no words having escape them yet.

"Well" he said, "there's good news and bad news".

"Oh for Goodness sake Griffin Dear. We don't have time for guessing games. Get to the point man – I'm sure whatever the situation is you are more than capable of dealing with it"

He nodded, puffing out his chest just a little at that last sweetener after her initial brusqueness.

"The downstairs is clear. But..."

"But they're surrounding the house and its falling down around our ears." I said chewing my lip.

Louise looked from Griffin to me and back waiting.

With a nod he told her it was true.

"How long do you think this house will hold up?" I said to Griffin. He shrugged, "if this were a normal house then it shouldn't be falling down at all."

"...but it not a normal house. It's a creation of the Keeper's unique mind and powers." Louise said, with a tut shook her head, "no, that's not it. He pulled the particles together from what was around him and rebuilt them into whatever he wanted to create. These walls..." She knocked with her knuckles. "This floor", she stamped on the rug covered ground, "actually exists. Otherwise we'd be standing among the scorpion snakes and walking into the light to meet our ancestors" She gave me a knowing smile.

"So," I said, "...how long have we got until this...collection of particles comes tumbling down, dropping Dorothy, the Wicked Witch and the Lion onto the pincers of the Scorpion Snakes," my frustration coming through just a little. Alright, a lot.

Louise's eyes narrowed, "I wouldn't call you the

Wicked Witch Dear and I'm just a little too old to be Dorothy...but I take your meaning...Dear."

Damn I was back to 'Dear'...that didn't take long did it?

As if timed, the roof shook, two perhaps three different cracks extending and intersecting to create a jagged circle in the wall, with a blink, it disappeared showing us the world outside as a huge piece of wall fell to the ground below with a loud 'currumph' and 'Squelch'.

The ceiling shuddered, groaning, collapsing inwards with a tumble of plaster and wood. It was literally coming down around our ears. We needed to find a way out and soon otherwise we'd be down at ground level and could count the rest of our life in seconds on a single hand.

"Unless we can get them to shoo then we need to find another way." Louise said, walking to stand in front of me.

I would have dearly loved to see her try to shoo them away, and a tiny part of me believed she had the force of character to pull it off. I know if I was a scorpion snake faced with Louise I'd be scared as all hell. Fact!

"Time I repaid the service you did for me Sam." Placing her fingers on each temple she put her face a few inches from my own. "You're going to have to let me inside your mind."

I disengaged from her touch, taking a step back. I'd been inside Louise's head, had in one instance occupied every thought and memory she had. I knew she was trustworthy but I couldn't bring myself to allow her in. I moved out of reach, shaking my head.

"After we're out of this house I'll let either of you figure out what your crazy friend may have done to me but...right now, I'm not going to let anyone else inside my head."

"But I..." Louise said but a new voice interrupted from the floor below.

"Is anyone up there?" I knew that voice.

"It can't be..." I said running to the top of the

stairwell.

Looking up at me from the ground below was a white toothed smile, a dark face and a beanie pulled down almost over one eye, a skateboard poking out from between the half closed zips of a back pack.

"Hey pretty lady," he said smiling up at me, his hands on both rails, "...thought you could you use a bit of help..."

"No, not really...we're all good..." I said chuckling and turning to a Griffin and Louise, her racking fingers through her loose hair in disbelief.

"Oh, in that case..." He turned to leave and with a laugh bounded up the stairs, two at a time grabbing me in a friendly bear hug, or probably more accurately, a werewolf hug. After a few bone crushing moments he released me, still laughing, and offered his hand, in turn, to the others.

"You know this place is surrounded by the weirdest..." Raul said like it was just an interesting fact instead of a desperate threat.

"How did you find us?" I said cutting him off, wanting to pinch him just to make sure. You can't blame me, I'd seen this house appear, disappear and reappear again, and now it was falling apart around our ears moment by moment. The edges between reality and imagination seemed a little blurry right now.

"You wouldn't believe me even if I told you..." He said scratching his head more vigorously. "Do you know this house is on the edge of Salem Acres?"

Griffin nodded but kept quiet, Louise shrugged. Both silent, probably wondering if they were better off with Raul or the creatures downstairs.

Salem Acres. I knew we'd driven outside of Salem and into the country but I'd been asleep, I wouldn't have known Salem Acres from any other collection of trees – to me they were just 'forest'.

"But Salem Acres is a big place." I said, the question still in my voice. "...and I didn't call you. I didn't even know I could call you."

Still scratching his head, he looked down at the

ground, hesitant.

"It was a...a little person." He said, mumbling almost too quiet for any of us to hear. We leant forward, making sure we'd heard right.

"A what?" Louise said.

"A What?" I reiterated in disbelief.

Nodding he looked up, his eyes looking to each of us in turn.

"I said..." His voice louder this time. "...It was a dwarf – you know a height challenged individual. Looked like he was dressed to go to a Lord of the Rings convention or something. Even had the green hat and the damned axe slung over one shoulder. Just seeing him made me what to sing "Hi-Ho", scared the hell out of me just appearing like that in the forest. Almost peed up a tree I can tell you..."

"You were wolf or man at the time..." I asked, a small smile on my face.

"Wouldn't have mattered, I'm just a wolf deep down...I'd have peed myself whatever. What Can I say?" He grinned back. "But the dwarf knew you. Told me you were in trouble and pointed in this direction. I've been running full out to get here since..."

"How did you get past the creatures?" I said checked him over, seeing if he had any cuts or signs they'd stung him. Nothing.

"Those weird snake things?" He said. "A few of them tried to sting me and I jumped back at first but then I just stamped my way through and risked it. Squashing as many of them as I could." He looked from me to Griffin and finally to Louise. "Why haven't you guys left already? The house is falling down, you all know that right?"

Louise bent down, pulling Raul's jeans to the side taking a look at a few puncture holes where the Scorpion Snakes had obviously stung his legs. Green liquid still running down his shins and staining his white sports socks.

Lifting her palm up to his head she stepped back, chewing on her bottom lip.

"You don't feel sick? Faint?" She asked, staring at him intently, looking for signs that he'd been affected by the stings that less than an hour ago had sucked the life essence out of the Keeper's body and turned him into nothing but bare bones.

"No. Why?" He ran his hands down his shins, then lifted his jeans to look beneath. "Why? I told you they didn't have any poison. Or if they do...it doesn't affect me."

"But that's...impossible isn't it?" I said to Louise and Griffin. Griffin stroked his chin, considering.

"Well, the fact that he's standing here says it's not impossible. Something I read somewhere..." He said, his voice trailing off as he thought it through, then he spoke up again. "Thiess. That could be it. Why didn't I think of it befo..."

The ceiling gave a last shudder and gave up pretending to be a critical piece of a house. Sending more dust and rubble into the room and before we could do more than gape, the whole ceiling pitched and fell inwards.

Raul half dragged half lifted us around our waists towards the top of the stairs, Griffin bundling up behind as we dived down the stairs.

I landed near the bottom, my hands skidding down the edges of the stairs. My hands out front trying to break my fall, before hitting the floor, I tucked my head against my shoulder letting myself roll, feet flying overhead.

Tumbling, I saw the hallway above disappear, plaster and wood following us down, covering our faces and hair in dust, splinters and grazes.

As the air cleared, we sat, Griffin rubbing his back and wincing, while I looked to Raul and Louise. We all seemed fine except the head to toe powdered plaster so we looked like a baker had dropped us in vat of flour before tossing us down the stairs.

Brushing the top of my head with my hand, a small cloud billowed into Raul's face, making him wince and cough.

"Well that was close" Louise said, "at least we're all in one piece". Standing, dusting down her skirt raising her hand to her mouth and giving a polite cough.

Remembering the layout of the downstairs I considered where my room had been, the floor having given way and dropping the scorpion snakes to the ground. We stood in the downstairs hallway of the gothic house, rough cut gray stone, the saint tapestries still hanging from floor to ceiling.

Two standing iron candlesticks swaying, matching chandelier swinging, white tallow candles making the dust sparkle as it floated through the room.

Directly opposite was the large wooden iron studded door, a heavy bar of oak stretching from one side to the other nestled in thick metal hooks. Thankfully there was no built in pet door, otherwise we'd be awash with little black beasties.

A last door lead into the rest of the house, open up any of the two doors and we'd be monster food.

But there was little choice. The upstairs of the Keeper's house had ceased to exist. This hallway was all that was left. It was just a matter of time, perhaps seconds, until these last few walls came tumbling down too.

We had to find a way out and now.

"Griffin, you mentioned Thiess upstairs." I said as I looked around for any stray flame throwers lying around. No such luck.

His eyes lit up.

"Yes, Thiess believed he was a werewolf." He watched Raul take an immediate interest. "A common belief is people become werewolves because of a curse or Satanic alliance."

Raul shuffled his feet, looked uncomfortable, and occupied his fingers by straightening his beanie. Griffin directly addressing Raul.

"I would warrant a guess that you are not the seventh son of a seventh son and have not pledged your soul to Beelzebub – am I correct?"

Raul stopped playing with his hat, glancing at

each of us in turn.

"If you mean Satan then no, never met the Dude."

"So how did you become a werewolf?" The ceiling we stood under cracked sending a new shower of wall onto Griffin's head. He glanced around nervously. "The short version if you don't mind." He said.

Raul's eyes darted up at the ceiling, then his words tumbled out...

"It came when I hit puberty." He glanced up at the quivering ceiling then back at us. "Some guys got hairs on their chest. Lucky me, I got them all over." He grinned before looking above again, nervous. "You won't believe this but I considered becoming a priest when I was younger." I heard a slight discord in what he was saying but filed it away for later

He looked at each of us to see if anyone found that thought somehow amusing. Him. The werewolf. A priest. Ha!

But I was certain all he saw was sympathy when he looked from Louise to Griffin to me.

For the first time in some time Griffin smiled, clapping Raul on the back.

"That all adds up Raul. That's what I was saying. Thiess."

Raul looked as perplexed as I probably did. We both gave Griffin a 'huh?' look.

Realizing we didn't have a clue who Thiess was, with an embarrassed grin,

"Thiess believe himself to be a werewolf. In Thiess' view, Werewolves were God's hounds, sent to combat witches and demons." He chuckled at the shocked looked both Louise and I must have given Raul.

Raising his hands Raul babbled "Hey, don't look at me. I like you guys..."

"That's why those Scorpion Snakes didn't affect him." I said having my own 'aha' moment. "He may not be anti-witch – but perhaps that's why the Keeper master was out to get him."

"...Because I can give him a hard time?"

"You could be the wrinkle in his plans...especially

if you're immune to his poisons," my words almost drowned out by the creaking and complaining of the walls baring the creatures from getting to us.

"Well..." I said, walking up to the front door and lifting the wooden bar. "There's one way to find out and it doesn't look like we have too many choices... Raul, can you come over here a second."

He stepped over a quizzical look on his face.

Putting my arm around his neck I jumped like a cradled baby into them, Raul grabbed and held me off the floor.

Pulling the front door open I sucked in a breath as Raul jumped though the gap. Pulling the door closed looked down. Scorpion snakes writhed in a frenzy around Raul's sneakers, their poison tipped stingers striking over and over, covering them with green liquid the color of Mountain Dew.

Taking a step with me in his arms, Raul's foot landed on piles of squirming creatures.

As his foot crunched down, Raul stumbled.

Chapter 48

If it had been me, Louise or Griffin instead of a werewolf with a heighted sense of his own physical form, that stumble would have pitched me to my death. As it was, his near trip gave him momentum. Raul half ran, half jumped forward, feet stomping down on creatures striking even as they were ground underfoot, his feet landing with wet crunches. Tightening my grip around his neck I could smell his sweat, feel his lungs pumping as he lifted me a little higher.

Looking over his shoulder, I saw his feet leaving a trail of white goo and fractured black shelled bodies like obscenely shaped smashed dark chocolates, off white fondant centers leaking out. But not for long, a blink and they were replaced by more manic creatures desperate to sink their stingers into Raul's flesh. It's not always nice to be loved.

Being held so close to Raul's chest I could feel his breath starting to labor. That didn't make sense given he'd only taken a few steps since we'd left the house. But as he moved forward he seemed to slow, his arms holding me lowering as if I were getting heavier.

Seeing Bessy, Griffin's green Morris Minor under the tree, I pointed. Gaining a new lease of energy Raul skipped forward, trying to touch the ground as little as possible. After years, we reached the car.

He smashed the front window with a quick elbow, held me with one arm, as he used the other to lift the lock. Throwing me unceremoniously into the front passenger side, Raul slammed the door before any creatures could follow.

With a grunt, he leapt upwards, disappearing as he landed on the roof of the car above me, the material of the car's ceiling bending inwards as he clambered to escape the stings. If we got out of this alive Griffin was going to be mighty pissed about the werewolf sized dent in his roof. I blew at my fringe.

Shuffling down in the seat, the upside down face of Raul looked through the broken window from above, his face looking sickly, a sheen of sweat across his cheeks and forehead.

"What happened?" I asked.

He swallowed, smacking his lips like he'd overdosed on Novocain at the dentist, his face pale.

"I guess there poison does affect me after all." He croaked. "It didn't kill me but boy do I feel like I've eaten some bad rabbit." Wiping a hand across his forehead and stared amazed at the film of moisture before, blinking, then blinking again, he seemed to pass out.

"Raul?" I said, sitting up. "Raul?" my voice rising as I reached out, tapping him gently on the cheek. Dammit! He was out cold. Peering down at the floor I could have sworn the little chitinous monsters chuckled, knowing sooner or later they'd find a way in and I'd be appetizer, entrée and dessert all at once.

I just hoped Raul didn't roll over or slide off. If he did then these flu type symptoms of his would get a lot worse, a lot more quickly.

Shit, shit, shit. What the hell was I going to do now?

This distance from the house I could see the whole Gothic mansion. It's walls had either completely disappeared in a pile of rubble or they soon would, it was unraveling in front of my eyes, like a house in a war zone and engulfing it, a demonic mind's creations. I was amazed the hallway was still standing, there was no reason why those walls were still there while others crumbled around them. One more minute and they'd be gone too.

Now what?

Chapter 49

"Raul?" I tapped his face, he moaned but stayed unconscious. Dammit, Dammit, Dammit!

"Raul?" I yelled close to his ear, this time turning up the swing on the face tapping. Alright, I admit it, I slapped him.

It didn't work. Still asleep. See, I told you slapping was useless.

Then I knew exactly what I was going to do.

Taking his head in my hands I lifted it, hanging half out of the window trying to ignore the intensifying clicking and chittering beneath me, I was just out of reach. The most eager lifted themselves higher, extending their poison tipped stingers in my direction but even the bigger of the creatures, some the size of Chihuahuas, could still not reach me.

"Ha! Take that you freaks" I said mumbling under my breath, just in case they understood English. Best not to taunt the murdering hells spawn of a demon if you want to see the back end of the teenage years is my philosophy. Well, it is now.

Turning my attention back to Raul I knelt on the car seat and knelt half outside the broken window grunting as I levered him fully onto the roof. Blowing my fringe, I slid into the car and looking back at the Master's animals, giving them a view of my middle finger and sneered. They probably didn't understand but it made me feel a hell of a lot better.

Lifting up over the gear shift and the metal handbrake, I shuffled awkwardly over to the driver's seat. Running my hands around the enormous black steering wheel, I moved the chair forward, dropped the visor, and caught the keys dropping into my hand.

Starting the car I searched to put the car into drive, down at my feet I saw one too many pedals. Slapping my head I cursed, I'd never driven stick shift.

I turned the key and smiled as Griffin's precious

1960 Morris Minor started without a hiccup.

Putting down the left peddle, moving the gearstick with my left hand, looked over my shoulder and gently released it to reverse. The car jumped forward, crunching as Griffin's classic car glancing off the elm tree.

"Crap" I yelled, banging the steering wheel, looking up, hoping I wasn't going to see Raul slid off the roof.

Hearing a groan from the broken window I shouted.

"You awake Raul...?"

No answer. Then I heard a tired voice saying "Yeah. Sam. That you? I don't feel too good."

"Can you get in here? I can help."

"I don't know. I feel kind of que..." He said, the volume of his voice going from soft to nonexistent.

"Raul?" No answer. Right. That's it.

Turning the key I jammed the gear shift down angrily and with that pressure something gave, needing that force. The car strained, inching backwards. Damn I think I found reverse. These English cars are weird man.

Looking again over my shoulder, my arm stretched across the back of the passenger seat, the car moved, whining as it strained to move backwards.

Fab, I had it in reverse. Life was good.

Smiling, I backed up, turning the wheel to line the front of the car with the house. As the car moved I heard popping.

A trail of broken and gooey creatures were left where the car travelled, it's small wheels taking out thirty, forty, leaving only perhaps thirty or forty thousand still alive. Small victories.

I pointed the car towards the last remaining walls of the house, and with a yell, one hand holding onto the handle above, drove straight at the house. Streaking across the distance I glanced out of the rear mirror smiling grimly as the car left two straight lines of chocolate fondant centered ectoplasm behind us.

Not watching where I was going was my one

hundredth or more mistake since this craziness started. Flicking back to see where I was actually driving, the house surprised me, I'd arrived and neglected to use the breaks.

Bessy hit the wall went straight through.

Reacting late, I pulled my feet off the peddles.

The car jumped and stalled, rocking forward and backwards. Out the side window I looked into a pink, shocked and angry face of Bessy's owner who looked like he was being strangled, his face moving through shades of red as he walked around Bessy, whimpers coming from his slack mouth.

Sticking my head out the window, I watched as Griffin crouched fingers probing where I'd hit the elm, a few twigs still lodged in the chrome bumper and to make matters worse, a lump of masonry sliding from the curve front bonnet leaving gouges in the apple green paint.

Racking his fingers through his hair he looked upwards, to find an unconscious Raul bending his roof inwards.

Louise walked over, her hand on the window's edge.

"Good job Sam. Stroke of genius to get the car through the wall." She said, glancing at Griffin. "We'd never had got to the car without being stung if you'd have parked outside. Genius young Lady, genius...".

With a hand on the back door she prepared to get in.

"Are you coming you old fool? Or are you going to continue to worry more about your precious car than the house falling around your pigheaded ears and you have seconds before you're snake food..."

That did it. Puffing out his cheeks, he pulled his trousers up a little and walked to the back of the car. Taking a hold of Raul he slid him off, caught him under the arms and lowered him slumping into the back seat beside Louise.

Strolling around to the passenger side he slid in, the car noticeably lowering, springs creaking.

Leaving me to drive.

All around us the walls shook, the car having taken away the last of the hallways integrity. It was unbelievable that, when every other wall and ceiling had disintegrated and collapsed that this hallway had remained. Incredible.

Preparing to backup, my feet flew from the peddles as something stabbed at my ankle. I sucked in a sharp breath as I looked down. A sole black Scorpion snake sat, its stinger devoid of green poison at my feet, its pincers spread wide and slicing the air with a repeated chopping motion.

With a scream I stamped over and over, my thick soled leather boots stamping the creature into oblivion, a sickly snot colored smear on the Morris Minor's carpet.

Then everything went black.

Chapter 50

A white dot appeared in the center of my vision, expanding and growing like a white blurry image was growing and travelling closer.

At first I thought it was a white translucent horse, galloping fast, puffing out clouds of cold breath, its hair flowing behind, but that imaged changed.

Next it looked like a man jogging towards me, tall, broad, wearing a leather jerkin, pointed boots a bow slung loosely across his shoulders. Robin Hood eat your heart out.

The picture changed again, shrinking, broadening, darkening. In place of that gorgeous hunk of a man stood a dwarf.

The dwarf.

Sauntering towards me a crooked grin across his still raggedly bearded face, his hair just a little greasy even as an entity I could partially see through. Great. Just who I needed to see as I slipped into the abyss, poisoned to death.

Yum. Aren't I the luckiest girl soon not to be alive?

"Well met Ms. Ray." He said drawing closer, rearranging the bow across his shoulders, the string tight across his chest and midriff. He saw me noticing and stopped, embarrassed.

"It seems a little tight on you." I teased.

He sucked in his gut a little. I couldn't believe it, he was a dead vain spirit. Perhaps after a few millennia he would realize he could change his spirit form at will.

"So why are you here?" I asked. "Come to gloat as you usher me in to the great beyond?"

Releasing his hold on his stomach it slouched back as he raised his eyes to mine. "You may not believe this but in my last seconds I..." He stopped talking, just looking at me with wide eyes.

I wasn't going to let him off that easy. Not even close.

"You what?" I took a step towards him. "You were sorry you Master betrayed you and didn't care that you died?"

Taking another step forward. "You're sorry you trapped and tried to kill two of your oldest friends as well as me?"

I looked down at him. "You're sorry you tried to pass on your Keeper responsibilities to me only to get me killed by one of your masters warped snake things? What?" His shade shook his head from side to side as I spat my words out at him. "What are you sorry about Mr. Damned Keeper?" Giving his spirit form a shove I raised my voice yelling. "You want me to forgive you? To say 'ah don't worry, these things happen?', surely you can't be that deluded? You died...what...an hour ago? And you've already lost touch with reality or maybe that's it? Maybe you never really had much of a relationship with reality after all- not surprising given you could create it at will..."

He raised his hands up in supplication, interested in his feet and afraid to meet my eyes.

I snorted. "I thought not, even in death you're a coward." calming down a little but not backing off, the fact I was here was his fault. "How could you?" I said, then dropping my voice down a notch "Louise and Mr. Griffin were you're friends. How could you?"

That brought his eyes up to mine.

"That's not the point. The Master is persuasive..."

"But you resisted for so long. You were the Keeper for...years and..."

"Centuries" he said interrupting me his voice sounding tired, drawn...heavy, "...Eons".

I didn't realize it had been that long. Having that responsibility for so long, it could wear anyone down. But that was no excuse Dammit! No excuse! Was it?

I looked at his face anew. The deeply etched worry lines spanning the corners of his eyes, the hard corners of his mouth, his brow. A weight had been placed upon his shoulders too many years ago to comprehend and in the end, he had buckled. Would I have buckled too? I could stand here and accuse but deep down, a doubt nagged at my stomach – I wasn't sure I could be strong every moment for centuries. Easy to say – but could I be sure I'd never make a mistake? – I hadn't done too well on that score even in the last week.

I gave him some space without me towering over his head.

"What now?"

He looked up. "Now?"

"Yeah – what happens now?"

He shrugged. "Well I'm dead. From what I understand since arriving what's going to happen to me is a pretty set process...I could tell you but then I'd have to kill you." Giving me an ironic grin.

I grimaced back, must be dead guy humor. Having just been stung to death by his Master's scorpion snakes, I wasn't seeing the funny side.

"Come on Sam – you can smile if you want to you know."

Was this guy mad?

"I don't want to."

"Sure?" that lopsided grin of his annoying me as he stood there, one hand on his hip. Then it occurred to me – he was playing with me".

"Alright – I'll bite..."

With a fake 'what me?' face, he paused then guffawed.

"You're not dead Sam." a wide faced grin answering the confused disbelief on my face.

"Not..." I scratched my head, my synapses not firing as I tried to digest what the Keeper was tell me. "Not Dead? But...the Scorpion snake..."

The Keeper laughed. "The scorpion snake?" He looked a little apologetic in an impish kind of way. "Yeah. About that..."

I glanced down at him, not liking the way this was starting to sound.

"About that?" I said wanting to drill a hole in his head with the squinting pupils of my eyes.

"Yeah. Um. Well. Truth be told..."

"Truth be told? What the hell is that supposed to mean? Truth be told..." I said, stepping up close and personal again, pissed.

"Yeah." He shuffled his feet, pushing his hands into the waistband of his trousers. " Er. That Scorpion Snake was...well, it was one of mine..."

I glared at him, raising my eyebrows to my hairline.

He tripped over his words in a gushing rush, "I needed to speak with you and I don't get visitation rights until I've paid off a few penalties. Should only take a decade or two but that would be too late...So if the mountain wasn't allowed to hang out with Mohammed..." pulling his hands free and spreading them wide as if saying the most logical obvious conclusion in any dimension.

So if I'm hearing this right, he can't get out for a day pass, so he thought he'd poison me and bring me through for a quick chat. Of course...makes perfect sense, to a deranged ancient supernatural demon's servant, sure. He was seriously deranged!

I peered at him from under my fringe. "So am I dead or not?"

Considering the point he stopped and grinned. "Not".

"Not. So why..." I gave my fringe a quick blow for good measure and considered kicking him in the groin again. "Why the hell am I here?" I said, trying to keep my voice below 'nuclear screech'.

Sensing my well hidden frustration he rattled out,

"We don't have long. If you stay too long then you might not be able to go back to your original body." He said. "We wouldn't want that would we..."

"Get to the point then", I growled, beginning to wonder–if what I dealing with to save a few lives was worth it...

"The house fell down after I died right?" He looked at me to make sure I was agreeing.

"So..."

"Everything except the main hallway, right? The walls have binding spells, reinforcing them. That because that's where I kept them. The Grimoire and the Voynich Manuscript".

Now I was interested. "Go on".

"Well, no one but me and..."

"No one but you. But you're dead." I said.

"Tell me about it. I tell you – the accommodation down here is..."

"Get to the point" I said, my fingers poised an inch from grabbing him by the neck and turning him into an ugly condiment shaker. I wasn't sure if I could do it, this side of the divide but I'd give it a damned good shot.

He looked at me from under a shaggy fringe "No one but me...and if you'd have let me finish..." a petulant whine in his voice. "...now you.... I designed it that way."

What the hell was he talking about? My close friends? This was getting weirder by the second.

"Where...are...the...books." My words spitting out between my grinding teeth.

"Can't tell you unfortunately. One of the rules of this whole dead thing. But I can give you a clue."

"You can't tell me because it would be breaking a rule. You're here because you broke every decent rule there is..."

Placing his palms together as if in prayer he rolled his eyeballs wide and sneaked a peek upwards. "I'm repentant. Even a wretch like me can be forgiven." Pulling his hands apart he glanced left and right in case we were being watched. I hadn't seen anyone or anything since I'd arrived here and was unsure whether there was even anything to see.

Seemingly satisfied at the lack of spying angels or whatever the heck he was expecting to see he leant closer.

"Let's get down to business. I'll help you get the Grimoire and the Voynich Manuscript but I need you to do something for me." He said, hope in his voice.

What could a recently dead dwarf possibly want that I could possibly give? Once I got my hands on John

Dee's Grimoire and even more important, the Voynich Manuscript, I was sure I could send his Demon Master ass back to the hell he came from. Whatever the Keeper wanted, there wasn't much I wouldn't give him.

He beckoned my down to his level.

Crouching down he took hold of the back of my neck, pulling my ear close to his mouth.

"Did I mention that when I died you inherited a few things? You can retrieve the Voynich manuscript and assuming you agree to our bargain you will forget this discussion but..."

"You said I'd be able to get the manuscript. What about Dee's spell book?"

The Keeper grinned.

"You don't have to worry about that. As I already said, I've organized it so only you have access – just like I did. It should appeal to a girl like you..."

His eyes glinting strangely, fingers spasmed before scratching at his wrist without realizing.

Before I could think of what to say next he moved closer, whispering the information I needed to retrieve the books, it drove out all the other questions out of my mind. Then he whispered what he wanted. Or more accurately, his two demands. The last made my face blanch as I absentmindedly blew my fringe with a half breath.

Oh Gods.

Chapter 51

I have never drowned.

I've never even come close.

But I've thought about it.

Sucking in a breath and finding the air has gone, replaced by fluid.

I knew I'd resist breathing. I'd hold my breath, my cheeks puffed out, my body shaking then spasming, fighting with me, demanding to breath no matter what.

Screaming inside my head, desperate for that one, extra, impossible to find breath.

Coming back to my own body after being...over there was like drowning...but in reverse.

My spirit could fathom how to breath, but the air was the fluid it resisted breathing in. My spirit or soul was forced back into the shell I'd thought of for so long as my body, it felt like an ill-fitting hazmat suit after having been a different form in a new dimension. I felt bulky, unyielding, suffocating.

I was drowning in my own body.

A fist slammed down on my chest and with eyes wide with shock, I breathed, coughed, puked and was alive again.

From a distance I heard Griffin speaking, his words feint.

"We have to take her to a Doctor Louise. She stopped breathing for at least three...maybe four minutes. We have to get out of here now."

There was some reason why we couldn't leave yet.

But I was too faint, in too much pain. I allowed myself to sink back into darkness.

A pair of small but immensely strong hands pushed me back towards Griffin's voice.

"We can't leave yet. John Dee's book and the Voynich manuscript are here... we...can't..."

Ignoring the sand and grit scrapping across my

eyeballs I opened my eyelids knowing exactly what I was supposed to do, I just wish I remembered how. The faint image of the Keeper's face flitted across my memory like the ghost of a butterfly.

With the right combination of word, will and action I imagined, gestured and created the glass case spiraling in a circle from the crumbling ceiling as if hanging from an invisible cord.

Snapping my fingers, the case fell to the ground.

With a gasp Griffin tried to jump forward to stop it crashing to the stone floor.

With the last of my strength I slowed its decent until, it seemed not to move hardly at all until, the very corner of the case touched the solid floor. A single crack appeared and ran around one side of the glass cube, as the two ends met, a large square fell to the floor splintering into a thousand shards.

Two books sat on a mottled brown leather cushion. One large, thick and crimson, its spine laced with thick cords, gouges and scars running crisscrossed across its cover, a knife shaped recess inset into the front cover.

The other was about six inches by nine, non-descript, plain creased and cracked brown cover speckled with black and grey which, from here, had a texture that made my flesh creep.

Louise reached in, choosing to pick up the larger of the two first, hefting it and whistling under her breath. Leaving it on the credenza she reached in for the smaller of the two, glass that had just crashed to the floor, crunching underfoot.

As her fingers brushed the edges of the second book, I crashed too.

Chapter 52

Pulling my face free from John Dee's Grimoire I woke up. The first thing I noticed was the empty hollow in its cover. I shoved it away before truly registering that it felt all wrong.

Head thumping stomach flipping, I reached my senses out towards it. It felt warped, oily and powerful. No wonder I had woken up as soon as I'd come into contact with it in the back of Bessy as I'd rolled around unconscious in the back.

Not having the willpower to move, I rolled my eyes towards the window and watched the oaks and elms alongside the road flash past, a blur of greens as we bumped and jumped our way back (I hoped) to civilization. Something knocked against the back of my legs, complaining I turned over hoping I wasn't about to meet the second Scorpion Snake of the day.

An unconscious Raul lay on his side beside me, rolling as the car moved, his beanie over one eye, his backpack beside his head, skateboard poking out the top.

"Hey." I said, tapping his cheek. "Hey...Raul. Time to get up Dude." Notice the skateboard speak, I too can 'hang' with the cool kids.

"Raul. It's me. Sam. Time to get up..."

He groaned, rolling onto his back, a floppy hand thrown across his face to partially block out the light.

"Just another ten minutes Ma." He said, his voice croaking, wincing as he massaged his temples.

"Not ten minutes Raul." I said, still tapping his cheek. "Now"

"I said...ten minutes." starting to get annoyed, waving me away, his eyes squeezed shut as he abruptly sat up., His head hit the top of Bessy with a thunk. Falling back he rubbed the top of his head groaning, eyes opened a crack, He looked to me, red rimmed and glassy.

"Ouch. Why didn't you stop me?"

I smiled. "Stop you from what? Carrying me like a hero to the car so we could all get away from those psycho creatures or stop you hitting your head on the roof of the car like an idiot?"

He looked rough, just like my Father did on a few rare occasions after getting together with his old Navy buddies.

Leaning up on his elbow, his thumbs and fingers massaging an eye each.

"The last one." He said quietly wincing, like every noise was a loud noise about to crack his head open...

"Anyway, thanks. We owe you one. How are you feeling?"

He gave me a twisted smile.

"How do I look?"

I whistled before telling him. "Wow. That bad huh? Guess the poison from the Scorpion Snakes does hit you after all. Lucky for you and us, it didn't kill you..."

"So, if doesn't kill me it should just make me stronger huh?" he said snorting, "somehow I doubt it. Anyway, I feel like I've had too much tequila and the worm at the bottom of the bottle tried to eat me instead of the other way around."

We travelled around a turn, the Morris minor leaning on old creaking springs, the crimson leather Grimoire knocked against Raul's legs. Laying a hand on its scarred cover, his fingertips trailed along a deeper gouge, he bent his head on sideways to read the books spine.

"What's this?" He said, looking up at me. "Yours?"

I shivered, just the thought of owning the book made me feel queasy. "No, belonged to a dead guy."

Closing my eyes I reached out with my senses, wanting to get a better understanding of the power within it. But no matter how I mentally tried to grab hold of it, it squirmed away, like two magnets of the same pole, pushing against each other.

It seemed to know I was testing it, sensed my need and was weighing me, responded, rebuffing me.

Could John Dee have protected it somehow? Perhaps a spell?

Cracking my knuckles I gave up on the subtle mental evaluation of John Dee's spell book.

Time for the direct approach.

Turning the book on its side I began to undo the leather cord strung like a shoe lace between the two covers, feeling a mounting apprehension. If Dee had placed a magical rebuff spell on the book, perhaps he cast another spell to stop anyone but him physically opening it.

Shaking my head and mumbling to myself as my fingers slowed, I reminded myself that the Keeper had read the book. That he'd used it to gain some meaning of the Voynich manuscript, he'd used the manuscript to help bring his master over into the real world. It was his master who had been responsible for the deaths of at least two girls who looked a lot like me.

My fingers slowed further, pausing as I reached the last two holes still sealing the Grimoire closed. It was decision time. Go ahead and open the book and check out what was inside or be cautious?

Looking up I caught Griffin's eyes looking at me through the car's rear view mirror, calm and piercing. Watching and silent.

You know, it's strange, if he'd have forbidden me I'd be pulling the leather lace through the last two holes and would be on the second line of chapter one. He was leaving it to me to make the right choice, which made me hesitate. My fingertips danced across the cover which looked like Freddy Krueger had taken up bedtime reading with John Dee's spell book.

"So..." Raul said, "Are you going to open it or not?" shuffling closer to get a better look. "We're all sitting here waiting for you to make up your mind..."

I hadn't realized. Griffin had been watching I knew that, but Louise had also turned in her seat. Raul sat licking his lips and pulling his knees to his chest, waiting. I toyed with the lace, looking at each of their faces in turn.

My shoulders felt heavy, I was tired. Really tired. It had been one hell of a week. First the deaths, the demon inside my head, the Keeper's betrayal and bringing Louise back from the brink of death and the Master's ebony creations that had nearly had us for breakfast and underlying all of it, fear...bucketfuls of fear.

"Why me?" I asked no one in particular my fingers playing with the edge of Dee's book. "What did I do?"

Raul shrugged, Griffin silent, never taking his eyes off me in the mirror, and then Louise spoke, shuffling in her seat, crackling as the old material moved with her.

"What did you do? Why nothing dear – this is a consequence of being a witch with real power." Her face serene but a touch sad, "and like most gifts, it comes with responsibility and..." She turned to look out the window, not meeting my eyes "...because I think you may be the new Keeper."

"Ah...I...wh...No, that's not..." I stumbled.

She turned back, locking her eyes on mine.

"What? That's not possible?" she said, cutting off my halfhearted denials. Even I knew the Keeper had done something to me just before he'd died, I could feel it but I hadn't had a chance to even consider what. Frankly the thought scared the freckles off of me.

"Dammit. Why me? Why not you? Or Griffin?"

"Who knows why anything happens the way it does Sam." Griffin spoke up for the first time, his deep voice calming, reminding me of my Father even as we rattled along the country road with two books that had the power to unleash who knew what.

"Right – what now?" I said, not opening the book but pulling the leather lace back through the holes, tightening the two sides together. I'd made up my mind for now. The grand book opening could wait.

Griffin put his eyes back on the road, Louise turned forward and Raul breathed out a big breath, like he'd been holding it for five minutes flat.

"I suggest we go back to Mr. Griffin's bookstore, get a better look at those books...and Sam" Louise said to all of us a once.

My stomach back flipped, did the splits and nearly puked all at the same time. I really didn't like the sound of that but even I wanted to know what the hell the Keeper had set me up for...I bit my lip, blowing my fringe and felt it rise while I unconsciously pulled the zip higher on my leather suit.

"Me too?" Raul asked, his tone suggesting he had other places to be, all of them out of this madness.

"You too" Griffin and Louise said at the same time, no argument expected or accepted.

"Oh crap" Raul said, his tone unsurprised, as he pulled his knees in tighter.

In silence, mulling over our own thoughts as we drove back to Salem.

Chapter 53

Pulling into Griffin's pre-war garage, Griffin got out and yanked open Bessy's back door. I sat still in the back, John Dee's spell book clasped tightly to my chest. Raul sat beside me in silence, he rocked slowly backwards and forwards, his arms still clasped tight around his knees.

Pulling open the door, Griffin and Louise stood outside, Louise holding out her hands for John Dee's spell book. I started to loosen my hands but a powerful need made me pull it tighter, like a child clutches a comfort blanket. It didn't want to give it up right now, not after all I'd been through to get it.

Eyes opened wide in surprise Louise dropped her hands to her side and stepped back, giving us space to climb out from the flat back of the Morris Minor.

"What about the brotherhood of Sammael?" I asked Louise as I climbed out. "Are we still hiding from those bozos?"

Tutting, Louise brushed her hands down her cardigan and pleated tweed skirt, straightening herself out after the journey. "They are not bozos dear, they're necromancers. But now is neither the time nor the place. If you know what's good for all of us. Put that..." Her head nodding towards Dee's Grimoire, my arms crossed across it. "Somewhere were prying eyes can't see it. Here..." handing me the picnic blanket from the back of the car.

Bozos or necromancers, same difference I thought, wrapping the Grimoire, feeling strangely needy of its contact after the tartan material enfolded the book putting a layer between it and me. A small part of me felt relieved. God, was I going mad under all this pressure? My head snapped towards Louise.

"We need to sort all of this out" I said scratching the crook of my arm absentmindedly. "It's not...good. We have pieces to puzzles we don't even know exist...it's all...screwed up."

She nodded and, taking me by the elbow, brushing past Raul, walking us towards Griffin's bookshop, Griffin and Raul tagging along behind.

We walked almost unconsciously bunched together, protecting the books we had brought back from the Keeper's destroyed home. It struck me we had formed a weird team of sorts; Raul the protector; Griffin, the voice of reason; Louise the bossy leader and, well, me. What did that make me?

The sacrificial lamb walking blindly to the slaughter? Was I being offered up? The third girl to be sacrificed to the dead Keeper's master? Would they do that to me?

What did I really know about any of them?

Griffin, Raul...Louise. Could I really trust them?

Gods my head hurt. I pressed my hand to my eyes, closing them for a second. My head down, the blanket wrapped book slipped against me, almost wriggling away.

Putting my arms tight around the bundle, almost squeezing the air from my own chest. Glancing at the faces around me as we entered Griffin's bookshop, the bell tinkling a tin welcome.

Chapter 54

Clumping up the stairs, I followed sullenly behind Griffin and Louise, doing my best not to fall. My head came above floor level. Raul following behind.

The last time I'd been here just a day ago I'd thought it one of the most beautiful rooms I've ever seen. High windows, varnished wooden floors, intricate rugs, leather and flower patterned chairs overlain with an intertwining smell of beeswax, pipe tobacco and lavender.

The room had changed.

It had lost its sparkle, its three dimensions of color, the smells, had paled. I looked around, wondering what had changed. The leather chairs where the same, the rung hadn't moved, the light still pulsed through the ceiling tall windows, the smells, were a little stale. Was that it?

I walked through the room, not noticing until I bumped against the draftsman's table. Wincing as the hard corner knocked into me.

The room was the same.

It was still perfect.

I knew what was different.

What had lost its sparkle.

Me.

Louise stood next to one of the book cases, silent, watching me.

Her voice resonated in my head.

'You're not alone in this Sam'.

A small tear dropped from one of my eyes, travelling in a fast moist line to my top lip. I hadn't even felt it well up, it had just appeared.

Taking the hardest steps of my life, I walked to Louise, my arms outstretched before I had even completely arrived.

"Take it." I said shoving it forward. "You have to take it. It's...already. I can feel it. It's..."

Shaking her head she took a half step backwards, her back jarring against the wall and window frame.

"I...can't." her hand raised, "I know you won't forgive him...but the Keeper, He was stronger than all of us." She said, her elegant fingers massaging her temples briefly. "He kept both books safe for centuries. It was only at the end that..."

"But I'm not strong enough. I've held it for less than a day and already..."

Griffin drew closer, never taking his eyes from the wrapped bundle, his tongue running around his lips, then his eyes caught Louise's. She didn't move, not one finger, not one hair. But still he knew, understood. Stepping back he shook his head, pulling his eyes away like they had been stuck on with superglue.

I looked at Raul, a question mark running through the creases in my forehead.

"Not me Sister." He said, his hands raised in mock surrender. "It's all yours."

"We each have our reasons why we cannot hold John Dee's book." Louise moved around me, a delicate finger touching my wrist. "But you should still try to hold and touch it as little as possible."

Spinning on one foot before I began to argue with myself under my breath, lifting the book while, pulling off the blanket. I sucked in a breath as I came into contact with the leather covers again, the scratched surface beneath the flat of my hand.

Standing on tip toes, I leveraged the edge onto the top of the bookcase. Straining on tip toes, tipped it. It balanced, swaying, for a breath, as I held mine. Hands still outstretched, part of me hoping, my teeth on edge, for it to fall back into them. The rest of me wanted to take it and scatter the pages to the wind.

As I had my back turned Louise, Griffin and Raul had sat. Strangely Griffin had gone back to the flower pattern chair, his pipe resting on the table beside. Louise on the broad high back leather chair, both hands stretched along its arms and dancing on their ends. Raul crouched on the foot stool his hands slack between his legs. He looked exhausted, still looking pale since the scorpion snakes.

Sitting opposite them all, I started asking myself questions before they even had the chance to open their mouths and do the same.

The Keeper had entrusted John Dee's book to me. I didn't know how attractive it would be to me as soon as I held it in my hands, it was compelling on a level beneath common sense and logic. I hated it, could feel dark tendrils passing through and around it, making my inner eye ache. But there was more, a different story. It called to me, demanding. Lucky for me John Dee or perhaps the Keeper had put a spell to stop others from gaining access. It needed to be bequeathed from one owner to another. As if reading my mind Louise smiled.

"So what do we know so far?" I asked, wanting to pull my thoughts away from the silent siren calling me just a step and a jump away. I dragged my eyes away and tried to keep them on Louise who sat with a look of supreme confidence on her face. Made my teeth grate. I started to look back toward...

"Sam. Sam." Louise's voice cut through the compulsion, a sliver of ice between it and me. Please pay attention dear".

"Sure. I'm listening" I said, a little sulky tone. So sue me, it's been a tough few days.

"So Sam asked us a question dear." She turned towards Griffin, who was busy lighting his stinky pipe. "What do we know so far?"

With a humph under his moustache, he prodded the tobacco deep into the bowl of his pipe. "Not a heck of a lot" he said, his fingers busy.

"Well we know Werewolves are to some degree immune to the poisons of the Keeper's master." her voice too chirpy, straining to be positive.

"The Keeper's master...Can we give him a name? Do we know his name?" I asked, looking from face to face.

Griffin voice rumbled, calm and deep.

"He's called Sammael." "Sammael" I said. "What

or who is he?"

"We don't know exactly who – we know why, 'Sam' means venom and 'el' means God."

"So we're dealing with some entity which considers itself the poison of God. Wow – talk about having a screwed up sense of your role in life." I said, kicking the table half-heartedly in front of me.

"It's not an entity dear. It's a demon..."

"Oh I'm sorry, a demon that believes it's the venom of God." I shot back. "Is that closer to the mark?"

"Perfect Dear" she said, sitting back more comfortably in her chair, an annoying half smile playing across her lips.

"And what does this demon want?" Raul asked, breaking the silent look between Louise and me.

Griffin sucked on his pipe, the flame of a lit match dragged downward into the tobacco while he sucked and thought through his answer. Pulling the moist end of the pipe out of his mouth,

"Well." He said "We've been through every book, every manuscript, and frankly every scrap of paper we can find and..." He sucked deeply on his pipe. "We can find no reference to Sammael needing sacrifices of red headed teenage girls or anything even remotely similar."

Louise interjected. "The most likely explanation is that Sammael and his disciples need the blood for some rite or other. But..." she drummed her fingers on the arm of her chair, "We are so completely in the dark, this is all just guess work."

Thinking back to the red haired girl outside the Bookshop of Horror and the other on Salem Common I shook my head. "I don't agree. They were just left to bleed to death after they were killed. You should have seen the pool of blood on my doorstep..."

"I agree with Sam." Raul said. "I found the girl on Salem Common, she was surrounded by blood. None of it had been taken or used as far as I could see..."

Griffin sucked on the end of his pipe not noticing that it had gone out. "Well, that rules that theory out."

"Well one thing we have determined is that the

Sammael was, for want of a better word, framing Raul for the murders."

I remembered the scratches carved into my front door and focused on what Griffin was saying.

"Our perhaps irrational explanation for that is Raul, as a werewolf, is one of God's hounds created to send demons back to the deepest rings of hell."

Raul shifted uncomfortably on the foot stool, obviously not appreciating being spoken about as if he wasn't here.

Louise stood, pacing around us.

"Sammael is so called for a reason. One thing it does well is poison. The fact that Raul..." She touched him briefly on the shoulder as she passed "...didn't die from the stings means there could be some truth in Thiess' theory."

"That means I need to be out front. One dose of Sammael's love juice and you guys would be playing backgammon with the skeleton I saw picked clean outside that creepy house." Raul said.

"He's right Louise." Griffin said, ignoring the reference Raul had made to the Keeper's dead body.

"I know he's right, Raul has some immunity. We'll need to take that into consideration as we move forward." Her fingers dug into the Leather arms, creating deep dimples she didn't seem to notice "I think it's time for us to consider John Dee's Grimoire and the Voynich manuscript."

My head pivoted to the top of the book case, then I remembered the other, less obvious manuscript, mottled brown, the texture of its cover reminding me of skin. It was strange I hadn't even thought of it once after touching Dee's book, it was almost as if it had fallen through a hole in my memory. Now Louise mentioned I could picture it, think of it, but before she had, it was if it had never existed.

"Where's the Voynich manuscript Louise?" I asked, my voice almost as low as my eyes from under my black fringe.

Blinking, she hesitated then reached into the folds

of her cardigan and held it up. I could make out its simplicity, no thongs, leather laces or bulls blood leather covering.

"From what the Keeper told us..." I said, my eyes never leaving it, "...he used Dee's Grimoire to translate elements of that manuscript. A feat no one has even managed before as it's written in a completely unknown language." I looked around at each of them, "Is that about right?"

"That's about right..." Griffin said. "...except you neglected to mention the Keeper used those translated elements to call Sammael to this world. Since then he and his followers have killed at least two girls that looked a heck of a lot like you and had some powers of their own..."

"And what about the sensation I felt when the Keeper died?" I asked. "He spoke of passing his legacy to me. Could this really happen? Did it?" Looking first to Griffin then to Louise.

They both cast silent glances at each other and I sat, waiting for some explanation from Griffin. Instead, Louise spoke first.

"The Keeper was unusual." She said hesitantly, choosing her words carefully. "Everything around us is made from elements on the periodic table...you know, Sodium, Chloride, put them together and you..."

"Salt" I said impatiently. Basic chemistry, I thought, tell me something I don't know.

"Well the Keeper could..." she licked her lips, "...go to an even more infinite level and pull these minute elements from his surroundings and recombine them. Like building a lego house at the molecular level."

"Wow, so the house we stood in that collapsed around us..." I said.

"That existed. It wasn't a vision or an illusion. He had literally built it molecule by molecule with his mind."

"His mind? You've got to be kidding? Can you imagine the power that must take?"

"No." Louise's voice deep and solid.

"No what?"

"No, thank the Lord, I can't imagine that amount of power. I'd be afraid to find out. I couldn't imagine the temptation if I possessed power like that?" She looked at Griffin, Raul then me. "Could you?"

Griffin kept his own council, his lips firmly closed, pulling in a lungful of smoke.

I pushed a little.

"When I asked the Keeper he said it was fairies that created the house. Is that possible?"

Louise shrugged. "Perhaps. Tell me what you felt when the Keeper died? What was it like?"

I thought back, instantly remembering the under the skin itches, the feeling like I was being radiated, glowing with the heat and power that was washing over and through me. If I had stood beside an X-ray machine which had gone rogue, juicing up its surrounding and everyone in it – that would be what it had felt like – down to the bone heat, straight under the skin and down into the very marrow of my skeleton. Remembering, my imagination worked overtime creating the sensation akin to termites walking around with heavy booted feet under my skin.

Pulling up the sleeve of my motorcycle suit I gave my skin a good scratch before pulling the sleeve back down.

"What about Roger Conant? We all saw him walking away with John Dee's spell book." I glanced up at the same book sitting atop the book case, it was undoubtedly the same just centuries older and more worn.

"Our order has had that book for centuries. When Roger died he secretly left it to his son, Exercise Conant. Before Exercise left Salem in 1694 he gave it to us, claiming the book should never leave Salem. We've had it from that time to now." Louise said, steepling her fingers in front of her chest in front of the glasses hanging from a gold chain around her neck.

"Did he say why the book shouldn't leave Salem?" I asked leaning forward, sensing we were getting closer.

"Well dear, obviously we weren't there but we've

been able to piece together notes written by our predecessors. There was some vague mention of the book and a knife in its cover, and the need for these items to remain within the boundaries of Salem. No mention of why but..."

"But it was clear to the order the 'book and the knife' needed to remain in Salem..." Griffin interrupted.

"Or?" I asked looking from one to the other and back.

They both shrugged, their faces moving from concerned to worry.

I paused, holding my breath as I thought it through,

"...and where is this...knife."

Griffin and Louise looked glum as they both sat back deeper into their chairs in silence.

"The Keeper had that too didn't he?"

It was a second or two before they both nodded, a first it was a slight recognition of the fact but then it was a true affirmation.

"And now it's gone? Was it in the house when it collapsed or..."

Hells bells, how could I be so dense?

It had already left the house, the Keeper must have given it up. The Girls...

We had the book but the knife was gone. I'd bet a lung Sammael or one of his disciples had their grubby little hands on it. But why?

"Griffin, you said there was no reference to Sammael needing sacrifices as a demon. Okay but are there any references..." I took a deep breath, collecting my thoughts just for a second, Griffin, Louise and Raul all looked at me expectantly. "...to blood being used to pull a demon into our dimension? Perhaps as part of a summoning spell?"

"Of course" Louise and Griffin both said over the top of each other. Griffin signaled with his hand, offering Louise the floor.

"Blood is a common element used when summoning a demon. But there's a lot more to it than blood. The girls that were killed, if it had been a summoning it would have been obvious."

"Obvious? How?"

Louise shifted uncomfortably in her seat, this was a subject she didn't seem to appreciate talking about.

"There's a...process for summoning. Each demon or summoned creature has its own seal and description..."

"Seal? What's that?" I interrupted.

With some impatience wanting to get this explanation over with as quickly as possible Louise answered, "Think of it as the demon's name. The seal is the demon's mark. You need to focus on the mark, to call out to the demon using invocations and then burn the seal. That's the basic way – if you are insane enough to try to call across a demon like Sammael you need at least two extra ingredients...enough Magic to power a small city and life force."

"...blood would be the life force, and the keeper..."

Griffin nodded. "To create material from the molecular level takes an unbelievable amount of power but where were the circles? The runes? The other elements to summon Sammael? What we have is a dead girl on a doorstep and another dying in Raul's arms. No invocations or spell used as far as I can see."

He was right. Neither of the deaths had any obvious signs that they were used to pull Sammael into our dimension. But there was something missing, some piece that would make it all clear. Then I realized just what was missing.

"It's the Knife."

There was silence as I stood, walked to the bookcase and hopped on one foot until my fingertips brushed against Dee's spell book, Griffin started towards me, but I pushed it back further and out of reach.

Stepping alongside me, Griffin reached up, "Allow me..."

"No" I yelled even before it registered in my own mind what I was saying. Gaining more control I lowered my voice, keeping it calm with some effort as, between teeth, I tempered my outburst.

"No, please. Could you...lift me...just a little? Then I can reach."

Scratching his head with a bemused look passing across his friendly face he hesitated a second then, pushing up his half-moon glasses he stooped, took a grip around my waist and with a slight grunt, lifted me from the floor.

I touched the spell book, a prickling feeling of painful pleasure passed through my hands, down my arms and through the rest of my body. Another object sat beside John Dee's book.

I looked at the increasingly pink faced Griffin,

"Mr. Griffin, could you move me closer...and a little higher."

Blowing, he lowered me as he crouched, getting his legs firmly underneath. With a small explosion of breath he hoisted me another foot higher than before. Letting go of the book I reached and grabbed. It was dusty. Picking it up I brought it under my nose to get a better look, it was a dried black bird's foot. I threw it to Raul who effortlessly snatched it from the air like it had never existed.

"Hurry up Girl..." Griffin said straining under my weight. Grabbing the book, my fingers naturally taking hold of the edges of the hole left now the knife was gone.

"I've got it. You can let me down now." I said, never taking my eyes from Raul who was examining the bird's foot, Louise looking over his shoulder, looking pale.

Landing on solid ground I tucked the book under my arm and walked over to Raul so I could get a better look. Louise stepped back, looking positively white.

"Why is that up there?" I asked. "It's not just a bird's foot Sam. It's a raven's foot. Ravens and executions go hand-in-hand." her eyes never leaving the dismembered foot sitting in Raul's palm. "It is said that when Walter Raleigh was executed in the Tower of London the Raven's went nearly mad with grief...I don't know how the foot got there but, death usually follows. Its possible Sammael's followers have already been here..."

She pulled her cardigan tightly around herself then signaled to Griffin with a gesture towards the backpacks we'd brought in.

"We need to leave. Now".

An itch appeared in an unreachable place between my shoulder blades. Gritting my teeth I helped the others pull a few bags together as quickly as we could.

Half a minute later we were walking out of Griffin's bookstore and into the last light of the day.

Turning the corner of the street the upstairs windows of Griffin's bookshop outwards with a detonation, followed by a green smoggy cloud bellowing into the street. The windows on the other side of the street shook, car alarms screaming up and down the street.

Hustling into the street beyond led by a puffing Griffin doing his best to get us away from whatever had decimated his shop.

Putting his arms around Louise and me, Raul two steps behind as we bustled forward hoping we were moving fast enough to escape.

Chapter 55

Twenty minutes of rapid feet movement, white faced perspiration and a significant amount of rubbernecking over our shoulders, we had collapsed inside the bookshop of horror.

Snapping on the light, I looked around at the piles of books, the half empty boxes and the thin layer of dust accumulating since I got diverted by dead girls on the doorstep.

Without waiting to feel the usual guilt, I pulled aside the curtain to the door to the Store's private rooms. Unlocking the door with the key hanging on a chain around my neck I ushered them through to the rooms beyond.

Having not properly moved in I made my excuses as we walked down the dark hallway towards the sitting room, avoiding the bicycle I'd leant against the side wall, ignoring the threadbare patchy carpet and the hint of damp left by the previous owner.

I dropped down onto the sofa and let John Dee's book fall with a loud 'thunk' amongst the coffee mugs and heat rings becoming part of the coffee table design.

Sammael and his boys seemed to know what they were doing and we were still guessing. We needed answers and like it or not, there was one place left that might give us the information we needed now the Keeper was a Scorpion Snake appetizer.

"We need to look in John Dee's book." waiting for some argument or alternatives from Louise...then Griffin...and last Raul.

There were none.

I wasn't sure if it was the shock of seeing Griffin's book store, exploding without warning or if they agreed but by the heavy silence which only seemed to get heavier as we sat.

"You all agree?" I asked, incredulous. I'd expected Louise would demand I leave it well alone.

Wow!

It was all on my shoulders.

Without much thought I responded to an itch between my shoulder blades while I made up my mind.

Licking my lips I scooted forward on the sofa my knees brushing against the edge of the coffee table, hands poised above the large crimson leather spell book that even now made my fingertips tingle, both attracting and repelling me.

Chapter 56

Like a giant carpet-generated electric shock, a jolt slapped my hands as they edged closer to Dee's Grimoire. Resisting the urge to pull my hands back to rub the prickly soreness out of them I moved closer, eyes wide with anticipation.

I stopped, taking a breath in case an alternative idea had magically appeared before I plowed forward.

Neither Louise, Griffin or Raul even noticed me looking at them for inspiration, each had their eyes locked on Dee's book, interest, need and revulsion passing across each in rotation. I pulled the leather laces through, ring by ring until, dragging the cord from the book, I lay it to the side.

A powerful itch ran up both my arms making me my hands tremor, wanting to do nothing more than scratch to relieve it.

Resisting I blew my fringe absentmindedly, my fingers caressing the front cover, an unmistakable indentation, a knife shaped miniature grave.

Taking hold of the books hardcover edge I lifted.

It refused to move, no flex or movement at all, locked.

Leaning down close, my eyes at book level I looked at it from all sides, looking for some binding, some strap that held the covers locked together. There were none.

Lowering his glasses down his nose Griffin spoke,

"I was afraid of that. The Keeper has put a binding spell on Dee's book. No one but the Keeper will be able to open it..."

"...and he's dead." Louise said with some frustration in her voice.

Those words ran around my head, I'd heard those sentences before but I couldn't...then an idea came to me from nowhere.

"Raul – do you have a knife?" I said, hoping I

wasn't going completely mad.

"No...sorry, never needed one." He said, and briefly concentrating, a single razor sharp claw protruded, pointing towards the ceiling with a slight curve, near invisible pink veins ran through it length.

"Would this help?" he asked holding it aloft.

Taking hold of his hands to keep it still I balanced my right palm on top of the nail. With a wince I dragged it across slicing into my flesh. Keeping the 'ouch' to myself, I closed my fingers and watched blood form at the bottom crease of my fist.

Ignoring the pain I held my hand above the space that had held Dee's knife. The first droplet of blood fell into the recess and was followed by more until a thick layer of my blood covered the place where the knife should lay.

Closing my eyes I concentrated, aware of my own blood that even now began to soak into the spell book, its own life force slowly dissipating like a nuclear isotope. For the first time since the Keeper had died, since I'd felt the all over body prickles as his power had radiated through me, I was using my power. The reality of what was happening hit me hard, my power immeasurably stronger, almost sickeningly so.

Diving into the very molecules of my own blood, I took hold of the intrinsic energy within it, opening my mind, told the book to open in John Dee's name. A mental lock giving way. I opened my eyes to focus again on the face of my friends.

"We can open it now." I said to each of them. "Are you ready?"

Louise and Griffin nodded, Raul shrugged, trying to seem cool and ambivalent. He didn't pull it off, he wanted to see inside as much as the others inching closer as he strained for a better look.

I knew how they felt.

This time it moved under my fingers.

The recurring itch started again, threatening to drive me crazy. I opened John Dee's Grimoire.

Chapter 57

Dust, mold and age billowed into my face as I pulled the thick leather covers apart, one side slapping the table as I let it fall. Separating naturally, the pages fell left and right, settling and deciding the two pages we should see first.

My stomach twisted as I caught glimpses of the pages as they fanned out. I had a suspicion and a sick feeling they were empty, each page perfect blank. After all we had been through, it was empty.

John Dee had been the spiritual advisor to Elizabeth I, he had passed his spell book onto Sir Walter Raleigh who had gone on to become a famous figure that changed history.

Unfortunately for Sir Walter he had eventually been decapitated in the Tower of London, his executioner a young Londoner was given Dee's spell book, probably more of a curse than a gift.

This young Londoner took the book to the colonies, eventually founding Salem, a city famous for Witches, spells and magic, the good and the bad kind.

Now, here we were, the book cracked opened in front of us. They were blank.

Completely blank.

Pages devoid of words, design or even the occasional scribble.

We had risked our lives to get this and the Voynich manuscript cradled in Louise's hands, as she sat, opened mouthed like the rest of us, trying to get our heads around the fact that John Dee's spell book was completely and utterly empty.

Scratching my wrist I yanked my leather sleeve up my forearm, nails relieving a built up tickling.

What the hell?

Just as I thought the pages had stopped moving, with one last burst the paper rustled, the pages jumped.

"Oh my God" I heard from across the table,

Louise was looking at what looked like two pages devoid of writing, but from here, it was empty except for brown stains and smudges. Blotches which, from this angle, looked like a string of islands across a monotone map, but even that was a stretch. To me they were just stains.

"What?" I asked as she reached out, her fingers moving towards the page as if pointing. "What Louise?"

Impatient, I turned it, wanting to see from the same angle as Louise.

The same brown stains, no logic or sense to them, then, as if rearranging themselves for my benefit. The smudges reordered and changed their alignment. Now it was my turn to gasp, the shapes congealed into a face. Smiling up at me, a roguish sense of humor clear on a one sided grin.

I stared.

Was this some sick joke?

Was it a last twist of the knife by the Keeper no content to betray us but needing, even in death, to ridicule and taunt us?

A hand settled on my shoulder. Pulling my eyes away from the grinning jokers face I looked into a face that was the Keeper's opposite. A caring and courageous man, Griffin had come around, placing a hand on my shoulder. "Don't worry Girl. There's more to this than a joke. I'm sure of it." his tone upbeat but thoughtful as he looked at the Keeper's shroud like image in the middle of John Dee's Grimoire. The spell book had caused the rise and fall of many men. Dee, Raleigh, Conant and the Keeper himself.

Now it was in my hands...and it was empty, except for the face of the betrayer.

Getting ready to slam the two sides of the book together in disgust, my teeth aching from being clenched together so tightly, they gained some relief as I choked as the Keeper's shroud image winking at me, his grin widening further than I thought possible.

Griffin's hand restrained mine fingers on my wrist, a touch which calmed making me hesitate from throwing the book hard against the wall and yelling like a crazed banshee.

"Wait Sam. Wait...I think..."

The Keeper's winking eye opened faint spider web thin lines and splotches appearing on the page below his face. Straining forward the hairs on the top of my head tingled as they brushed against Raul and Louise's heads as we moved closer.

Less than sixty seconds later and the scratches had joined together. Creating first unattached letters, then floating words and finally, full sentences.

Griffin's voice spoke from above my left shoulder as his face floated above all of us, looking through the gap to watch as the alphabet became an anagram, then a sentence and finally, a verse.

"I've seen that before." He looked a Louise who didn't look back, her lips moving as she read the words to herself. Waiting, Griffin read and re-read until Louise sat back on the edge of the sofa.

"But it can't be." She said, not fully able to look away from Dee's book. "There's no reason why..."

Rubbing his hands together enthusiastically Griffin paced around the coffee table smiling and chuckling to himself, moment or two later and he had our full attention.

"What is it Mr. Griffin?" Raul asked. I kept silent, still boiling that John Dee's book was basically empty, it was hard for me to put a coherent thought together...I was just too damned angry.

"It's the prophesy Raul" Griffin said, looking to Louise who sat back thoughtfully. "Our order was formed because of a prophesy. We never really understood its meaning."

"And we still don't" Louise said, interjecting.

Griffin nodded. "You're right but couldn't it...well, just look at her." He said, gesturing towards me with a pointed finger.

"There's no way..." Louise answered but I could see she wasn't so sure and by the way her eyes flicked around looking for trouble, she was shaken by the possibility. "I hope there's no way..." she said, her voice falling off a cliff into nothingness.

This 'insiders' discussion was starting to get under my skin,

"What prophesy? What does any of this have to do with Dee's book" I said, slapping my palm down on the grinning face of the Keeper who seemed to take the assault in good spirit. A tongue appearing and sticking out at me from the page. "I thought this freak was dead. Now he's giving me attitude from inside a book?"

I locked eyes with the Keeper and said the first thing that came to mind...

"You keep pushing me and I'll throw you and this book into the closest fire place." Looking up at Griffin and Louise I slammed the book closed ending that conversation with a semi-satisfying last word.

"Can someone please tell me about this prophesy or do I have to go and ask Sammael face to demonic pointy nosed face?"

Louise's looked tired and drawn, her voice small.

"As far as the standard history books are concerned, the Order of the Dragon was a political group in Hungary made up of Royalty and nobles. Its members were called '**Draconists**' – its members included Vlad Dracul or Vlad the Dragon..."

"You said 'as far as the standard history books are concerned...' what about the non-standard history books? Or better yet, what about the truth?" I said, my wrist itching uncontrollably. I growled under my breath, Raul pricked up his ears as if hearing a sound he understood.

Louise smiled wanly, knowing I'd pick up on it but making nothing clear cut and easy. "Are you sure you want to know?" her face rock solid serious. "If there is any truth to this prophesy and if we're close to seeing it fulfilled..." She paused. "...then you might be better biting your tongue, passing the book over to us and just..."

Itch, Itch.

Dragging up my sleeve I bit my lower lip and scratched.

"Problem?" Louise asked, then walked around

took my arm and turned it over.

Black shapes poked out just below my sleeve.

Black letters were tattooed and stretched from above my wrist. Yanking up my sleeve, they encircled my arm, covering almost every inch and stretched up beyond the edge of my jacket.

Screeching I pulled the leather until it reached my elbow and stopped. Peering closer, the black words were written in English, black scratchy quill letters wound around like I'd been used as a notebook by some freaky...and then it all made sense.

Griffin, Raul and Louse watched as I pulled down the zip of my leather motorcycle suit, I didn't even need to look down at the top of my chest, their faces said it all. With a view no one else had I saw down between my breasts, my skin visible beneath the white t-shirt. Pulling my shirt collar out, I peered down, the words stretch down and across my stomach and beyond.

After checking below various items of clothing, it was clear tattooed words and sketches covered every part of me except my hands, wrists and face. If I got naked you'd be able to read Dee's spell book from one side of my cover to the other in his black spidery handwriting.

"That spawn of a demon..." I hissed pulling open Dee's book, slapping each page down firmly until I came to the center pages.

The Keeper's face coalesced and laughed up at me.

Chapter 58

My breath came in gulps as I looked down at my forearms. Fresh black words and sentences wound like word chains around my skin. I'd been marked. The Keeper had the last laugh, he'd said that his power and Dee's spells had been transferred to me and only me and my close friends would have access. Very funny!

Dee's spells were indelibly written across my naked body, too damned right only I would have access to them. I frankly don't have much time for any other kind of close friends, what with trying to save lives and all.

A memory in the back of my mind tickled my consciousness for recognition, wanting my attention.

Focusing I remembered back to the images the Keeper had shown Louise, Griffin and me. Sir Walter Raleigh being given the spell book by Dee, walking from the bedroom, the book under his arm while he scratched. Dee lying back against his pillow, finally at peace and comfortable.

The visual fast forwarded and I was seeing Sir Walter passing the book onto his executioner. The look of relief as he bequeathed the book to another.

Finally Sir Walter's executioner, Roger Conant walking away, Dee's book clasped tight, his fingers vigorously rubbing the crook of his arm.

Now I understood. I had inherited the Keeper's powers because he had gained them from being the 'Keeper' of John Dee's spell book, his Grimoire. As it passed from owner to owner it had given them powers enough to allow them to take a place in history, to achieve great things but it had extolled a price. And now, without wanting it, without asking for it... it was my turn. I had Dee's spell etched into my skin and with it came its power. But it would be up to me if it became etched on my soul – as it had with the other Keepers.

The Keeper's face looked up at me out of the central pages of Dee's empty spell book – the words of power running across my own skin.

"You..." I said my lips pulled back in a snarl. "Someone pass me a match..."

"Wait Sam." Griffin said, turning my wrist over. "I'm sorry to say this might be how it works, it might be...necessary. It might be what we need to give us a shot at winning. Right now – we're out gunned." his face sad but firm, he didn't like this either. His down turned mouth told me how he felt – that's all well and good but dammit, he didn't have to be a walking magic encyclopedia.

Glancing down at the bearded Dwarf's face in the book he winked, the grin never leaving his face. After a few seconds, weighing up my options I could count on two fingers. Chewing my lip, I looked up at Louise, I could run or fight.

"Tell me about the prophesy." I said and sat back on the sofa, waiting.

Louise, her head bowed a little, seemed to concentrate on breathing for a few moments before she began to speak. At first I could barely hear her words as she started to speak of the Prophesy then that was all I could hear.

Chapter 59

"In the beginning of days there was Adam and Eve. In the beginning there was just one word and that was God. There was no need for language, for speech, Adam and Eve understood each other without sound.

In the garden, they did not need to till the soil, to plant, to use tools – why would they need to do these things when they could create at will, from nothing, from the very essence of the universe..." Louise said, her words hypnotic, strangely story like and rehearsed, as if passed down through the ages.

Pausing, I found myself leaning forward, needing to hear more. Raul and Griffin did the same on the periphery of my vision.

Calming, my breath half released as Louise's spoke.

"This is the history and the prophesy of our order. It is a purpose and a warning." She waited, then Griffin nodded, after a moment Raul followed and without really understanding why, I too nodded.

Satisfied she continued.

"Adam and Eve were given dominion over all living things. This dominion came in the form of power. To make and unmake with the thought, the word and the gesture. Despite being tempted by the demon serpent, despite eating from the tree of good and evil, of life and death, despite being expelled from the Garden, Adam and Eve did not lose the power of the thought, the word and the gesture."

Her words stalled, she rocked back in her seat, her eyes straining into the distance above our heads, like she was seeing beyond us, beyond the place where we sat.

I almost screamed. I needed her to go on. To explain more. I resisted grabbing her by the shoulders and shaking the story out of her, my lip bled as I bit into my lip.

"…the power of thought, the word and the gesture was taught to the Daughters of Eve and the sons of Adam, they called it Adam's language or the Adamical language. Adam was the first wise man, the first magi.

Over lifetimes, over generations his power to create was passed on, the word 'Adamical' changed - the use of thought, the word and the gesture as 'Magical' or 'Magic'. The gift given to Adam and Eve is the root of all we now consider magic. This was the root of our kind…"

She licked her lips, the words drying her out as she spoke. I wanted to urge her on, her words making so much sense, her explanation completing questions I'd had since I realized I was different. Since I realized I was a women with power, a witch. But I couldn't speak, afraid if I interrupted her, she would refuse to explain more. And I needed her too – more than I needed anything else. I licked my lips; all moisture in my mouth refusing to flow.

"Eve was not the first after Adam. Another was created. She was called Lilith, a demon of the night. She was the mother of all demons, she and her kind preyed on Adam and Eve's offspring and joining them were the fallen angels led by Azazel. The Fallen ones and the Demons embattled mankind, and our only real defense, the thought, the word and the gesture. But even our magic didn't prove to be enough. We gradually lost the battle, becoming enslaved or hybrids of the demons.

A cleansing came, the first apocalypse, the flood that came to the earth washing it clean of Lilith, her demon spawn and the fallen angels."

She took a breath, her hands wringing together, like she were washing them clean with an invisible bar of soap.

"They retreated to the next dimension…"

She shook her head from side to side, her lips pursed tight.

"No…this is ridiculous. Ridiculous. It's just a story. No one believes it…"

Louise…please" I choked.

She nodded, started speaking again. Quiet and hesitant.

"They…gave up the earth to Noah, his family and those creatures that were considered clean and righteous. They were saved from the first apocalypse of water. After 150 days of flooding, Noah's arc found ground. It was the beginning of a new world.

The world of mankind. But creatures had hidden in the darkness of the arc, stowaways. They had been made a promise by their Master and it was just a matter of time. They would work in the darkness to bring demon kind and the Fallen back to this earth – in time for the last apocalypse – a fire that would deliver a burning hell to the earth, finally cleansing the earth of Adam's decedents, giving mankind dominion over the earth once again. Unless…"

Louise slowly lifted her head, her gaze having fallen to the floor during her recital. Her skin pulled tight across the bones of her face, shadows beneath her eyes, triangles of darkness stretched to her jaw. As she spoke I watched the life draining from her.

"Unless…"

Griffin ran his fingers through his hair, looking decidedly uneasy as Louise ran her tongue around her lips, I could almost hear them cracking.

"Unless…Louise? Mr. Griffin?" I said, pleading to finish the telling of the Order's prophesy.

Mr. Griffin stood, turned away, not wanting to meet my or Raul's eyes.

Not knowing what else to do my fingers touched Louise's knee and with it she came alive again, clasping my hand in hers. Holding it tighter than anyone has ever held it before, crushed to her chest, her glasses splintering ignored beneath her fists.

"Unless the offspring of both Eve and Lilith willingly sacrifices themselves so mankind can once again pick a fruit from the tree of life." Louise voice trailed away, her last words muffled as she pressed our hands to her face.

The tip of my tongue touched on my lips, I tasted

my blood. It all made some sense to me, all except the sacrifice – how could the offspring of Lilith and Eve sacrifice themselves? Who were they and who were they supposed to sacrifice themselves too?

I needed more answers.

"Louise...Louise." My fingertips brushed the back of her hands, a small moan coming from beneath her hands, like she was complaining about being called upon again.

"Louise. Who are they? Who are the offspring of Lilith? Of Eve?"

Her hands shook, still clasped in front of her face. She dropped her fingers into her lap, her eyes red and worried.

"The offspring of Lilith?" She said, twisting her still covered face from side to side. "Lilith was a demon of the night. You would think of her offspring as...as vampires..."

Wow. Vampires? Am I hearing this right? Vampires, holy or rather unholy crap.

"Err, they're real?"

Louise nodded, a tear at the corner of her eye.

Made my flesh crawl to know they weren't some imaginary creatures with a fetish for bow ties and cummerbunds. I'd have to digest this later.

So a vampire would need to sacrifice itself for mankind...interesting.

"...And Eve?" I asked.

Silence. Louise kept silent, her eyes wide and white.

"Eve was the first true witch, the first female of the thought, the word and the gesture– the first Keeper of the Power. And you are the last...you and a vampire must sacrifice yourselves to save us all from the last apocalypse. If you don't, we're all dead and Lilith and the Fallen will have the earth as their playground once again."

Her words hollowed out my chest, making me want to run and hide, to stand up and fight all at the same time. I felt sick and nervous. Louise stood and walking over she put her arms around my shoulders, clasping me to her as she whispered in my ear.

"You must sacrifice yourself so that the rest of mankind may live. That is your destiny."

I swallowed, her words hard to hear.

"But that's not right...it can't be. I'm only Seventeen..."

She nodded as if that wasn't as crazy as it sounded, even to my ears.

Louise stepped back, holding my shoulders in a firm grip.

"You're right child. We'll do everything we can to stop that from happening. We'll find another way. Don't you worry dear..." She said, her hands patting the top of my head as she clasped me to her bosom again and for the first time since I met her, I didn't mind being called 'Dear' – it was the only constant in a scary world of nightmares.

So ends A Natural Born Witch.

THE END

Virgin Vampire; Werewolf Crusader and Witch Apocalypse – coming soon. Read about the author on the next page…

About the Author

Some people write books to become rich and famous. Others write books because that's what they do, they're writers. I write because I have some stories to tell – stories which have been kept in the darkness for too long.

Forgive the fact that there's no photo – the last thing I need is for people to recognize me.

The people who publish this manuscript did so at my urging. I passed it to them through a friend who guaranteed my anonymity. When you've had the kind of life I've lived, privacy is all I have left – aside from the nightmares to keep me company. A cold sweat urging a night shiver as the memories fade back into the depths.

I have some stories to tell. It's up to you whether you believe them. I recommend you take them with a pinch of salt or better yet, pour as much salt as you can find all around you in an unbroken circle and hope that will keep you safe. Maybe it will. For me, it didn't work.

If you want to know when the next story is coming, sign up here:

http://www.AntPublishingHouse.com/samray

www.ingramcontent.com/pod-product-compliance
Lightning Source LLC
Chambersburg PA
CBHW060134130626
46556CB00006B/2342